A Glimpse of Heaven on Earth

Paul gasped with pleasure when he reached the crest
of the hill and discovered the heart of the Napa Valley
nestled below him, spread out like a magnificent
Persian tapestry. Following the contours of the
terraced hills, dappled golden and red by the setting
sun, was an endless sea of lush vines, heavy with their
bounty of bursting purple grapes.

The air was softly scented with the perfume of the
grapes, intoxicating his senses. He felt as if he were
perched on the edge of paradise: he wanted to
memorize the vista, to remember that such extraordinary places existed in the world.

Victoria came to stand by his side. "We call it *Las
Nubes*," she said softly. "In Spanish it means 'the
clouds.' "

A WALK IN THE CLOUDS

A
WALK
IN THE
CLOUDS

A novel by Deborah Chiel

based on a screenplay by
Robert Mark Kamen
and Mark Miller & Harvey Weitzman

Ø

A SIGNET BOOK

SIGNET
Published by the Penguin Group
Penguin Books USA Inc., 375 Hudson Street,
New York, New York 10014, U.S.A.
Penguin Books Ltd, 27 Wrights Lane,
London W8 5TZ, England
Penguin Books Australia Ltd, Ringwood,
Victoria, Australia
Penguin Books Canada Ltd, 10 Alcorn Avenue,
Toronto, Ontario, Canada M4V 3B2
Penguin Books (N.Z.) Ltd, 182-190 Wairau Road,
Auckland 10, New Zealand

Penguin Books Ltd, Registered Offices:
Harmondsworth, Middlesex, England

First published by Signet, an imprint of Dutton Signet,
a division of Penguin Books USA Inc.

First Printing, April, 1995
10 9 8 7 6 5 4 3 2 1

 REGISTERED TRADEMARK—MARCA REGISTRADA

Printed in the United States of America

PROLOGUE

Victoria Aragon had a favorite story, one her mother had told so often during her childhood that she remembered it word for word, as if she had memorized it from a book. Some people might have called the story a fairy tale, because her mother always began it the same way.

"A long time ago," she would say, "in a country very far away from here and now, a brave and handsome *caballero* set out to find his own true love."

Victoria could see the *caballero* as clearly as if she were staring at his photograph. She could see him saying good-bye to his family, his mama and papa, sisters, brothers, grandparents, his brown eyes flashing in the sun as he took one last look at everyone he loved, all that was familiar to him.

"He sailed for many days across the wide blue ocean," her mother would continue, and Victoria would imagine him adrift on the sea, "all alone in the world except for the enormous white-winged birds circling over his head and the water creatures playing in the wake of his boat."

The story never changed from one telling to the next. The details were always the same.

"The *caballero* carried with him a compass to set his course, a map of the sky to guide him across the vast expanse, and a telescope to bring the stars closer so that he could more easily recognize the constellations that would lead him to his destination. Day after day, he faced terrible dangers—hungry sharks, fierce winds and rainstorms, crackling bolts of lightning, waves higher than the mountains he'd crossed on his way to the ocean, even a band of pirates who threatened to toss him overboard if he didn't surrender every last piece of the gold his grandfather had given him to buy a horse and seeds to plant in the New World."

Snuggled in bed, her head in her mother's lap, Victoria would shiver with fear that perhaps this time, somehow, the *caballero* would not survive the perils he faced. Her mother would stroke her hair and smile and go on with her story.

"Many times, the *caballero* wondered whether he would live to see the next sunrise, but he never lost hope. He always remained brave and resolute, determined to reach the far shores and the beautiful young *senorita* who awaited him there."

The story always ended happily, of course, as fairy tales should. But it was years before Victoria fully understood that the story was more truth than fiction—her mother's romanticized version of the journey her great-great-grandfather had taken to claim the bride his parents had arranged for him to marry.

If only she could have known him, that handsome *caballero* whose aristocratic Spanish blood flowed in her veins. He must have been so dashing, so adventurous, so resolute about creating a new life for himself in that faraway, foreign land called Mexico. She admired his courage. She envied his freedom. She wished she could meet a man just like him.

CHAPTER

· 1 ·

Paul Sutton had dreamed of this day for months. He had pictured it a thousand times in a hundred different settings: marching in a column of troops through the rain-soaked tropics, doing night guard duty in a jungle so dense with vegetation that he couldn't see two inches in front of his face, dodging bullets and enemy patrol units. He had painted the scene in his mind like an artist, filling up his mental canvas, coloring in each detail of his imagined home-coming.

One thought had kept him from going crazy during the darkest hours of the war, especially in the last few agonizing months of brutal combat when rumors had circulated that the war could very well drag on for at least another year or two. One thought had kept him company, warming his bones like a thick woolen blanket when he'd felt as if he couldn't stand one more minute of the wet and mud and fear and loneliness.

Betty was waiting for him at home. The sure knowledge that eventually he'd be returning to her—to his *wife!*—brought a smile to his face even when he was surrounded by an entire unit of Japanese with reinforcements two days away. He'd dreamed about her at night, conjured her up in his fantasies by day, recalled the smell of her perfume, the sound of her voice, the way she felt when he touched her, the look in her eyes after they made love.

Now, in just a matter of minutes—an hour at most—he'd be seeing her again. Peering over the side of the behemoth troop transport ship that had been his magic carpet back to San Francisco, he tried to pick her out of the crowd milling about on the dock below.

Except for the weather, the scene was just as he had envisioned it. Though he'd lived there long enough to know better, in his mind's eye the sun was always shining in San Francisco. Today a hard rain was pouring down, and a thick fog obscured the Golden Gate Bridge that soared above the harbor, connecting the city to rural Marin County and the wine country farther to the north.

It mattered not a bit that the rain had been falling since the early morning, drenching anyone foolhardy enough to be outside for more than a couple of minutes. Hundreds of women stood huddled under a canopy of black umbrellas, waving and screaming up at their husbands and boyfriends. A military band added to the noisy celebration, playing a medley of rousing Sousa marches interspersed with patriotic favorites by George M. Cohan and Irving Berlin.

The sun was setting behind the cover of dark clouds, the light rapidly fading. But neither the rain nor the deepening dusk could dampen the spirits of the poncho-clad soldiers who were gathered on the deck, while the ship was being properly moored and the gangplank put in place so they could begin to disembark. Paul squinted again through the mist, still hoping to spot Betty through the gloom. He'd written her the date of his arrival, and though he hadn't heard from her in some time, he was sure she was waiting on the dock to greet him.

Impatient to see her, he pulled out the photograph she'd given him as a good-bye present when he'd been shipped overseas. He'd carried it with him in its protective silver case everywhere, even into battle—the talisman that had kept him safe and brought him home unharmed.

"To my husband, Paul," she'd signed it with a flourish. "Your ever-loving Betty."

Lord, she was pretty! He would never forget the moment he'd first laid eyes on her at the USO dance—the smile on her face as she handed him a glass of punch, her auburn hair falling in waves down her shoulders like Rita Hayworth's. Somehow, he'd summoned up the nerve to ask her to dance, and she'd said yes. She felt like an angel in his arms, not seeming to care that he stepped on her toes, holding him tightly when the lights went dim and the band played "Goodnight Irene" to signal that the evening was coming to a close.

He glanced up and noticed one of his shipmates staring over his shoulder at Betty's picture. He smiled, acknowledging the other man's approving glance.

"When's the last time you saw her?" asked the soldier.

"Our wedding day. Four years ago."

Earning his chestful of medals for bravery under fire had required far less courage than asking Betty to marry him. He'd known her only a short time, but his unit was set to go overseas, and he couldn't risk losing her. She had made him the happiest man in the world when she'd accepted his proposal. He still couldn't believe his good fortune. He could see nothing he had done to deserve the love of such a wonderful girl, a jewel of a girl who dazzled him with her quick tongue with high spirits.

Like himself, she was a newcomer to San Francisco, recently arrived from northern Idaho where her people were potato farmers. But at twenty-three, just a year younger than he was, she was too eager for new experiences to stay on the farm. She wanted to see the ocean and travel, the broaden her horizons and improve herself.

He admired her energy and ambition. He, too, had a restlessness in his soul that yearned to be satisfied, which was why he'd moved out west in search of adventure. The war had provided plenty of that, to be sure. But late at night, too tired to sleep even after a full day of slogging through the war-devastated New Guinea countryside, he faced his deepest fears and discovered that what scared him most wasn't the prospect of death but the thought of dying without having ever really lived.

He'd been sleepwalking through life up until now, but the war had shaken him out of his stupor. If there was one lesson he'd learned on the battle-field, it was that a person could cease to be in less time than it took to look through the sights of his rifle, take aim, and fire. He'd survived the war. Now he had to grab hold of his future and make it work for him, instead of the other way around.

He knew Betty would understand. He'd poured his heart out to her in his letters, confiding in her his hopes and dreams and concerns. He couldn't wait to talk to her, share his plans with her face-to-face, begin to carve out their life together.

"Lemme guess," said the fellow next to him. "You met her on Friday. Married her on Sunday. Shipped out on Monday."

Paul grinned. "Pretty much."

"Me, too." The young man lit a cigarette. "Ain't war shit? I'll bet we don't even recognize them."

Paul looked again at Betty's picture, which he'd studied these past four years like an obedient pupil until her face had become as familiar to him as his own. The war—or perhaps it was destiny—had brought them together. Nothing would keep them apart.

He shook his head. His shipmate couldn't have been more wrong. "I'd recognize her anywhere."

It was already drizzling when Victoria Aragon left her apartment that morning. But she was late for class, and retracing her steps up four flights of stairs for her umbrella hadn't seemed worth the effort. Dashing to the library at noon, she'd regretted her decision. The heavens had opened up as they seldom did this early in September, dumping torrents of rain and creating coursing streams of water at many of the campus crosswalks.

By the end of the day, trudging up the street toward her building, she was drenched to the bone, thoroughly exhausted, and feeling just a little bit sorry for herself. This time of year was when she most missed her family, most keenly felt her self-imposed absence from her home in the Napa Valley. No one was forcing her to stay in San Francisco, certainly not her parents, who would welcome her back with wide-open arms.

It was she who had insisted on going to graduate school. She had made up her own stubborn mind, as her papa reminded her every chance he got. They'd fought bitterly over her decision, as they'd fought over so many things in the last several years. But Mama had somehow persuaded him to let her continue with her studies. Victoria couldn't even imagine what Mama had promised him in return for his consent. She knew he saw no point to her getting a master's degree. Papa had her future all planned out for her—and a career teaching English literature had no place whatsoever in his grand design.

He, especially, would have liked nothing better than to hear her admit how homesick she sometimes felt when she thought about all of them gathered around the table at dinner, making plans for the upcoming grape harvest. Her mouth watered as she pictured the heaping platters of chicken and vegetables served up nightly at the Aragon table, and she realized suddenly that she was not only cold and soaking wet, but also very, very hungry. Hurrying up the stairs, she hoped that Tom had stopped to buy food on his way home from school. He was so distracted lately that he could easily have forgotten, and then one of them would have to venture back out into the storm if they were going to eat tonight.

She fumbled for her keys but couldn't easily find them, so she knocked on the door. When she got no response, she sighed and shifted her books to her other arm, then managed finally to find her keys at the bottom of her purse.

"I'm home!" she called out, trying to sound more cheerful than she felt.

She was greeted by silence. The apartment was small, only one room, a tiny kitchen, and the bathroom. She saw at a glance that Tom wasn't there. A second, more careful gaze around the room, and the smile she'd put on for his benefit faded from her lips.

Something wasn't quite right about the place. Something felt different. She pushed a strand of wet hair away from her forehead and stared at the walls, which they had painted themselves when he'd moved in with her. There were empty spaces where Tom's framed posters of Paris, London, and the English Lake District should have been. She closed her eyes and took a deep breath, telling herself that he must have had a very good reason for taking down the posters.

But when she opened her eyes and saw that his books were missing from the bookshelf—all his volumes of Wordsworth, Keats and Shelley, his well-thumbed *Canterbury Tales,* the complete works of Shakespeare, his Fitzgerald and Hemingway novels—she could think of no good reason except the one that set her knees to shaking as she ran across the room to the closet.

Please, God, don't let his clothes be gone, she offered up a silent prayer as she pulled open the closet door. As usual, the left side was filled with her dresses, skirts, and blouses. But except for one white shirt, its collar frayed and soiled, all of Tom's shirts and pants were gone. So were his two tweed jackets with the patched sleeves, his extra pair of shoes, his raincoat, and his battered briefcase.

It was the rejected white shirt, hanging alone and exposed, that brought the tears to her eyes. She blinked them back in a determined effort not to cry and took a step or two in the direction of their dresser. But she couldn't bring herself to open his drawers, because she couldn't bear not to find his underwear and socks jumbled up next to the coins he emptied out of his pockets each night.

Suddenly it seemed very important that she remember exactly what she and Tom had talked about that morning. She'd gotten up first, as usual, and made their coffee, steaming the milk just the way he liked it and bringing his mug over to their bed, where he lay with the covers over his head. "Thanks," he'd mumbled, turning over to reach for the cup. He'd grimaced as he pulled himself up into a sitting position. "Headache," he'd said. "Must have drunk too much wine last night."

"I'll be home by six," she'd said and bent to kiss his lips.

It was hard to leave him these mornings while he was still in bed and all she wanted to do was curl up next to him and spend a few lazy hours watching him mark papers until he left for his noon class. But she didn't want him to worry that she was becoming a burden, or to think she was losing her passion for English literature, which was what had brought them together. So she smiled, kissed him again, and said, "If you pick up a chicken, I'll cook."

"Sounds fine," he'd said, so absentmindedly she wondered whether he'd heard her.

"'Bye," she'd called out of the apartment, but he was already engrossed in a book and didn't bother to answer her.

It had been different in the beginning, when Tom had tried every which way he could to get her into bed with him and keep her there. He'd read poetry to her—Shakespeare's love sonnets, Keats, Shelley, Wordsworth, even Yeats sometimes when he was particularly feeling his Irish roots—wooing her with the words that both of them so deeply admired.

He'd taken her out for long dinners at a smoky, dimly lit Italian restaurant in North Beach that consisted of nothing more than six or seven tables decorated with red-checked cloths and centerpieces made of candles stuck inside wax-encrusted Chianti bottles. They'd talked about literature—he'd talked, she'd listened—over plates of fried calamari and spaghetti, washed down with glasses of red wine that seemed far more intoxicating than what was served at her parents' table . . . or perhaps he'd poured more of it than she was used to.

Waking up next to him in the morning, she refused to feel ashamed or let herself think about what Papa would say if he knew what she was doing. She was twenty-two, no longer a child, and she shouldn't have to answer to her father about the choices she made. Boys her age were being sent overseas to fight for their country. The rules changed during wartime. Or so she told herself when she couldn't sleep in the middle of the night and lay in the darkness, watching Tom, wondering whether the two of them would ever understand each other as her parents seemed to do.

Her mother had only to give her father a certain look and he would nod or frown or smile, as if he could read her mind, and no words were necessary to say what needed to be said. It was different with

Tom, perhaps because he had been her teacher first, then her lover. But where was he now? Where were all his things?

She tried to push away the panic that was enveloping her like the fog that rolled in each night over the bay. Wispy fingers of fear trickled the back of her neck as she looked around the room, searching for clues that would explain his absence.

An envelope lay on the mantel over the fireplace. It must have been there all along, but somehow she had missed seeing it until now. "Victoria," Tom had written on the front, with two neat lines scored underneath her name with the red pencil he used to correct his students' papers.

Her hands were trembling as she tore open the flap and removed the letter she found inside. Tom's words leaped up at her from off the page. His message was short, no more than a sentence or two, but it said enough to break her heart. This time she couldn't hold back the tears that filled her eyes and spilled down her cheeks. She sank onto the bed, sobbing as she read and reread his terse good-bye.

It was all her fault. She couldn't blame him for leaving her. If she had tried harder, been smarter, more attentive, given him more of what he'd wanted. . . . She had done her best, but it hadn't been good enough.

She might have guessed it would end this way. He was so much older, wiser, more experienced. She was just a child, playing at being an adult, wanting so badly to prove to her father she wasn't a little girl anymore. And now what would she tell him? How would she ever explain to him what had happened?

The questions frightened her, and because she had no answers, she wept until her eyes felt raw and swollen. When she finally stopped, after a very long time, she looked up and realized that she was sitting in total darkness. Outside, the pale twilight had faded to night, and the rain was still falling, the water lashing sideways against her windowpane.

As she stood up to turn on a lamp, her glance fell on the collection of photographs she'd brought from home and arranged on her dresser: the one of herself surrounded by her family, standing near the house, and behind them the lush vineyards rolling endlessly to the horizon; herself and her grandparents, dressed in the traditional Mexican charro outfits that were part of their heritage; herself in her cap and gown, taken on her graduation day, with her father posed next to her, staring unflinchingly into the eye of the camera.

Alberto Aragon wore his aristocratic heritage proudly, like a priceless piece of jewelry that demanded recognition, both because of its inherent beauty and because it had been preserved over the course of so many generations. That he was a force to be reckoned with was evident from his posture, so rigid and uncompromising, and in his stern, unsmiling face. Staring at the picture, she remembered that even on her graduation day, which should have been her moment of glory and recognition, she had felt as if she were standing his shadow, diminished by his much more imposing presence.

She would have to tell her family what had happened. A shudder went through her as she imagined her father's reaction. He would be furious with her, full of harsh, blaming words. He would never understand. He would certainly never forgive her.

She groaned weakly as she suddenly felt a twinge of pain in her stomach, followed by a wave of nausea so intense that it sent her flying into the bathroom.

"Mama," she whimpered, crying again as she knelt over the toilet bowl. The sounds of her retching filled the silent apartment. "Dear Lord, help me, please, tell me what to do."

The dock area had gradually emptied out. The crowds had departed, the couples paired off under their umbrellas, gone to celebrate and get reacquainted. Even the band members had finally stopped playing, packed up their equipment, and left for the day. The street lamps that bordered the perimeter of the harbor had been switched on, and circles of light illuminated random sections of the huge map of the United States that had been painted over the concrete surface in anticipation of the soldiers' return.

Paul had spent the last several hours elbowing his way through the mob, craning his neck to find Betty, grinning with excitement as he tapped on the shoulder of one woman after another who turned out not to be his wife. Now, tired of standing but still hopeful she would soon show up, he sat down on his duffel bag to wait for her.

Five minutes passed, then five more, then another ten after that. The rain had let up for a while, but the sky remained overcast. Puddles had formed here and there across the map, and where the light intersected with the pools, he began to see drops of water gently rippling the surface as the light sprinkle threatened to give way to a heavy downpour.

Paul hitched his collar up around the neck, considered retrieving his poncho from his bag, and decided it wasn't worth the effort. He yawned and blinked his eyes, which felt gritty with fatigue. He scanned the road that ran alongside the dock, picturing Betty running toward him with outstretched arms. Could he have missed her earlier among the throng? He shook his head. Surely she would have waited if she hadn't found him. He tried to come up with some good reason why she hadn't yet arrived, but the various choices were much too worrisome to consider for more than a second or two.

The rain was coming down more persistently, and he felt the damp seeping through his uniform and into his bones. He hauled himself to his feet. It was time to get moving. If she turned up, she'd know where to look for him. He'd spent too many days and nights overseas with the rain pouring down around him, staring at the horizon, waiting out the storm, waiting for the war to end. What he wanted now was to be inside, at home, where it was warm and dry.

The neighborhood beyond the harbor was teeming with reunited couples, hugging and kissing as they walked arm-in-arm through the streets. It was Christmas, the Fourth of July, and a big-top carnival all rolled into one exuberant festival of homecoming. Weighted down by his disappointment, Paul slung his duffel bag over his shoulder and wearily plodded up the steep hill, sidestepping the happy lovers who were oblivious to anything or anyone but each other.

Their happiness was a stinging reminder of how lonely he felt, the odd man out among so many joyous revelers. His solitariness was an old and familiar condition, one he recalled all too vividly from a childhood spent too much alone. He'd assumed that marriage would protect him from meeting up again with the twin demons of sadness and grief that had accompanied him through so much of his life, that having a wife would be a magic charm against melancholy. But Betty was nowhere to be seen, and the demons were whispering in his ears, planting seeds of doubt and trepidation as to whether her love for him had outlasted their separation.

By the time he reached Betty's building, where he'd spent one blissful night after their hastily arranged wedding, his mouth was dry with tension.

He took a deep breath as he opened the door to the building and made his way up the stairs to her apartment. One thing hadn't changed since he'd last been there. The place was still a dump. The stale odor of cigarette smoke lingered on the landings, the hall still looked dingy, the paint peeling off the walls. He pulled out the silver case that held Betty's picture on one side, her key on the other.

He sighed as he stared at her picture, barely visible in the dimly lit hall. Would she be there to welcome him? How would he find her if she weren't? What would he do without her? The smile on her full, very kissable lips seemed to mock his questions, daring him to unlock her door and face down his worst fears.

As he fit the key in the lock—he was relieved to discover it still worked—he heard what was unmistakably a man's voice coming from inside the apartment.

"I find the pheasant to be quite pleasant. How do you find the wine?" asked the man, speaking in the sharp precise manner a person might use to address someone who was hard of hearing. His accent sounded strangely exaggerated, almost as if he were a miscast actor playing a haughty blue blood.

Paul was even more startled when a moment later he heard what sounded like a very distorted version of Betty's voice responding to the man's question.

"I find the pheasant to be quite pleasant. I find the wine to be extraordinarily fine," she said, obviously imitating the man, yet speaking in a manner both solemn and serious.

Utterly perplexed, Paul pushed open the door.

Betty stood next to a phonograph, clutching a book in one hand. "Omigod!" she screamed.

"I prefer to dine at home alone," declared the man, his voice booming forth from the phonograph.

"Betty?" Paul stared at his wife. She was dressed only in her bra and slip, but her face was made up with lipstick, eye shadow, and rouge, as if she were on her way out for the evening.

"Do you plan to summer in Cannes?" the man's voice droned on.

The book dropped to the floor. "Paul?" she said disbelievingly.

He put down his duffel and took another long look at her, trying to find the wife he remembered, the one he knew from the picture.

"Paul!" she cried, having finally grasped that this was her husband, come home to stay. She flew at him, wrapping herself in his arms.

"The pralines and creams are smooth as a dream," the man's voice droned on in the background as she covered Paul's neck and face with kisses.

Paul bent to kiss her lips, then buried his face in her hair. "When I didn't see you on the dock," he said, his voice breaking, "I thought . . ."

"I didn't know you were coming," she whispered. She pushed herself more tightly into the circle of his embrace and found his mouth with hers.

Her kisses were everything he had dreamed about during all the many months he'd been gone. But before he could fully give way to his passion, he had to quiet the demons and ask her why she hadn't met him at the dock. "Didn't you get my letters?"

"Oh, Paul, I started to read them," she said, tucking her hands beneath the jacket of his uniform. "I did. But after the first few, I couldn't bear to hear about the fighting and killing."

He shook his head, not understanding. *The first few?* But what about all the other letters? There must have been hundreds of them, pages and pages of his most fiercely felt longings and desires. "I wrote you almost every day."

"I know, I know." She nodded eagerly and twirled away from him. "I kept them." She pulled open a drawer in the cabinet under the phonograph and showed him four candy boxes he'd given her as gifts, jammed inside, filling up every inch of the drawer. The tops were held in place with brightly colored ribbons, one of which Betty unfastened now in order to open the box.

"Look," she said, pointing.

The box was filled with a stack of the letters he'd sent her. He was stunned to realize that she had never even opened the envelopes.

His surprise must have shown on his face, because she hurried to explain the lapse. "The thought of you in all that danger . . ." She pressed her fist to her mouth and shivered. "It was too much. I knew that if I got them that you were still alive. That's all I cared about, that you were alive . . . safe. . . . That's all that was important to me." Her eyes widened with concern. She clutched his arm and gazed up at him. "Can you ever forgive me?"

"Uh, sure." He suddenly felt very tired and confused. Nothing was turning out the way he'd expected it to. Of course, it was wonderful to see her, and she was clearly thrilled to have him back, and her kisses were every bit as exciting as he'd remembered them. But he'd imagined her reading and rereading his letters, reacting to whatever he'd shared with her, loving him more with each passing day. And now to find out that she hadn't even known when his ship was arriving!

"I wrote to you. You got those, right?" she asked anxiously.

"I got a few." He studied her face, trying to figure out what else was not as it should have been. Her hair . . . she'd done something different with her hair. It had been reshaped and cut into a short bob. The reddish-brown waves that had fallen down her shoulders were gone. She'd been transformed into a platinum blonde.

Misunderstanding his silence, she pouted and said, "I told you I wasn't a big writer."

Suddenly, Paul became aware that the record was still playing, the man's statements providing an inadvertent commentary on their conversation.

"I quite agree the distinction is dubious, don't you?" the disembodied voice asked now.

The man, whoever he was, had said enough. Paul moved the phonograph needle. The voice stopped, and the room fell blessedly quiet.

"It's a course I'm taking in self-improvement," Betty quickly explained. "He's wonderful . . . so smart."

She showed him the book she'd been reading: *Speak for Success*. Paul stared at the picture of the author on the cover. Armisted Knox was a jowly-faced man with a receding hairline who looked to be in his late thirties. Armisted Knox didn't strike Paul as someone who seemed all that successful. But when Betty put the book back on the shelf, he noticed she had at least a half dozen other titles by the haughty-voiced Mr. Knox.

"Oh, Paul," she said, falling back into his arms. She kissed him again, even more hungrily than before.

He felt himself relaxing, his spirits reviving. His doubts fell away as he began responding to her very insistent tongue and lips. He pressed her to him, loving the feel of the silk slip crushed between his fingers. He'd been waiting for this moment for so long.

But just as he was groping to undo her bra strap, she pulled away and took a half step backward. "You haven't changed a bit," she whispered, caressing his cheek.

But she had changed. "Your hair," he blurted out before he could stop himself. He missed her old look. He wanted her still to be the girl he'd left behind—the girl in the picture he'd carried with him overseas.

She proudly patted her blond curls. "It's the latest. Don't you just love it?"

"I kind of liked it before," he said, trying to mask his dismay.

"Oh, Paul, don't be such an old fuddy-duddy," she scolded him.

He stared at her, wondering whether she was right that he was making a fuss over nonsense. Long hair or short, Betty was a knockout, an irresistible vision of feminine curves and soft skin and silky underwear. And yet . . .

She smiled coquettishly and crooked her finger. "Come here." She put her arms around his neck and drew him toward the bedroom.

He felt almost dizzy with lust. But still he resisted, struggling to match this new version of Betty with his memory of the woman he'd married.

"No, I mean it," he said weakly. He groped for an explanation, driven by his need for her to understand even a little of his confusion. "I liked your hair . . . the way it felt, the color, the smell."

She nuzzled his ear with her tongue. "Don't you like the way it smells now?" She rubbed her hair in his face as she teased his shirt out of the front of his pants. "Don't you?"

He was panting now as she undid his buttons and unbuckled his belt. She flattened her fingers against his belly, stroking ever downward, laughing softly as she felt him growing hard beneath her touch.

She was his every sexual fantasy come true, his wife as seductress, pushing him past the brink of awareness. He felt himself sliding into a haze of desire. Her mouth was moving across his bare chest. His blood was pounding in his veins until he thought he might explode.

"I'm just saying . . ." He stopped, trying to recapture his thought. The rest of the sentence eluded him.

"Saying what?" she murmured. "Tell me."

Her tongue hovered just above his waist, tracing circles against his skin. His legs felt like rubber, threatening to give way beneath her touch. He wanted to sweep her up in his arms and throw her onto their bed and devour her. But a voice from deep inside himself still demanded to express itself.

"That just because something's old . . ."

"Yes?" she prompted him.

His head was spinning. He hardly knew what he was saying, or why. "It doesn't have to be forgotten," he stammered, hearing the words as if from a great distance.

"Forgotten." She echoed him softly and then, without warning, her tongue stopped moving and she pulled away from him. "Forgotten . . ." she muttered. "Almost forgot . . ."

It was as if an electrical switch had been thrown. She jumped up so abruptly that he almost lost his balance. Without another word she ran into the living room.

"Betty?" Dazed from the sudden transition, he lurched after her.

She was leaning down, pulling something out of

the cabinet. When she turned around, he saw that it was his sample case, the one he'd used before the war as a sales representative for a chocolate distributor. The company name and logo were emblazoned across the front of the case: SWEENEY'S SWEETS.

Under other circumstances he might have been touched that she'd saved the sample case, a souvenir of his life before the war. Perhaps she was wanting to show him she hadn't forgotten their briefly experienced common past. He appreciated the gesture, but her timing was off. If there was any reminiscing to be done, let it be about the fun they'd had together, not about his dead-end job peddling chocolates on behalf of George Sweeney.

The bulge in his pants was rapidly shrinking. "Betty," he said, ready to resume where they'd left off.

"It's another one of Armisted's courses . . . on memory," she explained briefly. "You hear a word, and you associate a thought. Forgotten . . . forgot . . . forgot to remember. Here."

Words? Associations? Forgot to remember? He didn't have the heart to tell her he was utterly befuddled. She may as well have been babbling in Chinese for all the sense he could glean from what she was saying. What was the connection between the mysterious Mr. Knox and the sample case, and why had she chosen this moment to dig it out?

He blamed himself for going on about her hair. The waves would grow back, the color would return to normal. He should have kept his mouth shut and made love to her, which was all either one of them really wanted to do right now.

She handed him the case with a smile. "I went to see Mr. Sweeney to make sure he held your job like he promised. He said you could start the day you got back."

She mistook his shocked expression for gratitude.

"Of course, I negotiated a raise," she said proudly.

He balanced the sample case across the palms of both hands. It was about the size of an oversized book, a volume of the encyclopedia perhaps, and even full of chocolates, it didn't weigh much more than a couple of pounds. But in the two years that he'd represented Sweeney's, selling the line to the candy shops and five-and-dime stores in all the dusty little towns between Sacramento and Stockton, the case had begun to feel like an anchor dragging him down toward oblivion.

He was a damned good salesman. George Sweeney had said so himself when he'd presented Paul with a fifty-dollar bonus for signing up more new accounts in one year than any other salesman in the state. People always said he was a likable fellow. The ladies, especially, seemed to like his smile, and he always made sure to show his manners and thank them kindly for their time.

But he'd come to believe that he wasn't destined to live out his years extolling the virtues of nougats, cherry centers, and marshmallow fudge.

She was looking at him so expectantly, waiting to

be thanked. He didn't want her to misunderstand. He wasn't unappreciative. She'd meant well. But her efforts had been misguided. He sighed and put the case down on the cabinet. "Betty, I don't know if I want to go back to selling chocolate."

"You have something better." She made it sound more like a statement than a question.

"No. But after what I've seen in the war . . . I mean, it gave me time to think . . . about life . . . what it means." He shrugged. It was too much to explain now, when they should have been making love, making up for what they'd missed. "I wrote you all this," he said, hearing his unspoken resentment.

She heard it, too, and stepped closer to him. "You want me to read those old letters?" she said softly. She rubbed her face against his chest, pressing her lips against his skin.

The resentment faded and gave way to confusion. His letters added up to the sum total of an experience he'd mistakenly believed he was sharing with her. Impressions, fragments of dreams, fears, hopes, memories, and expectations . . . he'd held back nothing, so convinced had he been that she was pouring over every page. He'd expected to return to someone who knew him, knew his heart and his soul.

Before their hastily arranged wedding, they'd been together for all of . . . how long had it been? Five weeks? A month? Probably not even as long as that. He'd been so sure about his feelings, but now he suddenly couldn't remember what had drawn him to her. And what had she seen in him? he wondered.

A good provider? A soft-spoken kind of guy, steady as a rock, someone she could depend on? Yes, he supposed he was all of those things. Or maybe she'd been seduced by his uniform and all the hoopla about the war, and the romance of committing herself to her brave soldier all those thousands of miles away.

He was not as innocent or trusting as he'd once been. Four years of soldiering had changed him from a boy into a man. He'd told Betty he loved her and couldn't live without her. But what if neither statement were true? That possibility was too awful to contemplate. He had nothing else—no family, no job prospects except for Sweeney's, not even a place to live besides Betty's apartment.

He looked over at the shelf, at the neat row of Armisted Knox books, each one offering the promise of self-improvement. He thought about his letters just as neatly stashed away in the Sweeney's candy boxes he'd given Betty while he was courting her. If only, he thought wistfully, she'd found his opinions as interesting as those expressed by Mr. Knox.

She took hold of his left hand and played with his wedding band, as if to remind him of the vows they had taken.

Did he want her to read the letters? "No," he said. The truth was he didn't know what he wanted right now. "It's just that you'd understand a lot of what I'm feeling . . . what I want."

"Sweetie." She ran her lips up and down his finger. "Tell me what you want."

He shrugged. "I don't know. I thought we could take some time off, drive down the coast."

She smiled indulgently. "Honey, cars cost money. Everything costs money, and we don't have any money. But we will, won't we? The whole country's making money hand over fist. You've been away, you don't know, but you will." She pressed herself against him, and very gently nibbled at his neck and shoulders, tickling his collarbone with her tongue. "Don't you want money, honey?" she said softly. "Tons and tons of money? I do."

"I thought . . . some time . . ." His voice trailed off. He felt her hands moving down his body, and then his arms were around her and he couldn't think or speak for wanting her.

She tugged at his waistband and stroked the V of flesh just below his belly. "Time's money," she whispered. "I want things, Paulie. My whole life I've been without. Don't you want things?"

"Yeah, sure," he said hoarsely, his legs gone to jelly. "But a little time . . . would be . . ."

She was like an explorer, venturing into his most sensitive, hidden places, claiming them for her own with her fingers. "What? Tell me," she urged.

"Nice," he breathed, caressing her hungrily.

"I'll give you nice, like you never had. All you want . . ."

He groaned as her hand found its mark and pushed him beyond rationality into a realm of pure sensation. Overwhelmed by the intensity of his need, he scooped her up and carried her into the bedroom.

He fell all over her, craving the taste of her skin, inhaling her scent. She moaned as he positioned himself astride her, but just as he got ready to enter her, she opened her eyes and pushed him back with the palm of her hand.

"We're gonna have everything, aren't we?" she coaxed. "Aren't we?"

She pulled his head away from her neck and forced him to meet her gaze. Her nodded, hardly having heard the question. In that moment he would have said yes to anything she'd asked of him.

Then he slipped himself inside her, his gasps of pleasure echoing hers as he yielded to the hot, fierce demands of their lovemaking. Conscious of nothing but the point at which their bodies had become joined, he clung to her. Her hands were knotted around his tautly muscled back, and she matched his thrusts with her own frenzied rhythms.

He cried out in ecstasy as they hurtled together toward the dark empty space where there was no holding back, no boundaries to their passion. Finally, they had become one again. But their union had to do only with the primal needs of the flesh. It had nothing to do with love.

What a fool she'd been to ignore their comments, which she'd attributed to jealousy. Flattered by his interest, she'd naively believed his promises and trusted that he would marry her. No, she corrected herself as she threw back the covers. It was not naiveté but stupid pride that had allowed her to ignore the danger signals. She was as arrogant as her father, convinced that whatever had happened in the past with those other girls, Tom felt differently about her. She was, after all, special. *She* was an Aragon.

She thought she might faint when her feet hit the floor. She had to rest for a minute before she was able to stand up and move about the room. She was hungry . . . ravenous, really, and with good reason. She'd felt so ill the night before that she'd had nothing but a few crackers and some sips of ginger ale before she'd gotten into bed and fallen asleep from the sheer exhaustion of so much crying.

Now her stomach felt queasy again. She quickly fixed two slices of bread and jam and forced herself to eat every bite, washed down with a glass of milk. No matter what, she had to stay healthy. She would need all the strength she could muster for the trip ahead, at the end of which she would have to face her father's wrath.

Her family was expecting her to come home for the harvest. She'd tried to put them off, using her papers and exams as an excuse. They'd ignored her protests and reminded her that she'd never missed the harvest, not even during her four years of college.

Her brother was coming up from Stanford. They wanted and needed her there, as well.

She had decided sometime in the middle of the night that there was no sense in her staying on alone in San Francisco. She would leave today, as soon as she was packed, and be home by evening. Perhaps all the fuss and bustle of the preharvest preparations would distract her father and protect her from the full fury of his reaction.

It was early, not even six o'clock yet, the sky just starting to lighten from purple to a paler blue. She pulled out her suitcase and began filling it with her clothes, books, and linens. She hadn't brought very much with her when she'd moved into the apartment. The few dishes and pots belonged to Tom, and the furniture had come with the apartment. She would leave it to him to sort things out with the landlord. That much responsibility she hoped he could shoulder.

A couple of hours later, she blinked open her eyes and found herself fully dressed, slumped in the chair next to the bed. She looked around, bewildered, then realized she must have sat down to rest and nodded off with exhaustion. Her heart was pounding, as if she'd been running hard, and suddenly she remembered the dream from which she had forced herself awake, whimpering for her mother.

A soldier had been chasing her through a forest. He must have been German, because he'd been shouting at her in some language other than English as he thundered after her through the dense, swampy underbrush. She knew he would kill her if he caught her, and her only hope was to find Tom, who was waiting for her somewhere nearby.

To her left, through a clearing in the trees, she saw a river, and on the other side a lovely old house surrounded by bowers of grapevines. A group of people was picnicking on the lawn that sloped down to the river's edge, laughing and enjoying the beautiful afternoon, totally oblivious to her danger. She could hear the soldier's footsteps pounding after her, close enough that she could almost see his face.

She waved her hands to get the attention of the picnickers and screamed, "Where's Tom? Tell him I need him!"

One of them stood up and called out to her, but she couldn't make out his words. All she could hear was the soldier, behind her, yelling, "I'll kill you! You deserve to die!"

She stumbled over to the sink and drank a glass of water. Then she looked at the clock and saw that she would have to rush in order to catch her train. She was almost done with the packing, except for her family's photographs, which she'd saved for last. She wrapped them one by one in a scarf and carefully laid them across the top of her clothes.

"Papa, please understand," she whispered, stopping to stare at her graduation picture.

Alberto Aragon glared back at her, grim, imperious, disapproving. His was not the face of a man who would ever understand.

* * *

A tangle of sheets that smelled of sweat, perfume, and sex. A girl sprawled next to him in bed, asleep, her short blond curls strewn across the pillow. Sunlight streaming through the window.

A collage of unfamiliar sensations took shape in Paul's prewaking mind, jarring him into sudden awareness of his surroundings. He was in San Francisco with Betty. Their wild lovemaking had gone on for what must have been hours. They'd finally fallen asleep, almost gasping with exhaustion.

Their clothes were scattered all over the floor. He eased himself out of bed and hunted down his skivvies, socks and shoes, shirt and pants. A quick shower and shave, and he was ready to go. And all the while Betty slept peacefully, hardly stirring even when he stubbed his toe on the corner of the dresser and let out a loud "Ouch!"

He checked himself in her full-length mirror to make sure his tie was straight and was momentarily startled by his own reflection. The mirrors in the barracks gave back such a blurry distorted image that he'd gotten used to shaving and combing his hair almost without looking. He hardly recognized the tall young man in the uniform who gazed back at him through the glass. Not a bad-looking fellow, he decided. Even-featured, nice brown eyes, hair still a little short from his military cut, but it would grow back soon enough.

He attempted a smile and managed to depress himself even more than he'd already been feeling. He scrutinized himself, chagrined by how clearly his unhappiness showed in his expression. Who was this guy with the sad eyes and droopy lips? he asked himself. The answer came back: salesman, husband, soldier, dreamer . . . and now, once again, salesman. But the deeper, truer truth eluded him.

He supposed Betty was right. A car, a trip down the coast . . . these were luxuries that cost money. Still, he hadn't intended to exchange his army uniform for a salesman's suit quite so quickly.

He straightened his tie, saw that he was missing a handkerchief, and went looking for one in the cabinet. He found a pile of them there, nestled next to the candy boxes that contained his letters. It struck him then that as little as he knew himself, he knew Betty not at all. They were two strangers who had shared a few meals, a few dances, a few hours in bed. Now came the hard work of getting acquainted with each other, finding out what the other was really about. And what if they didn't like what they discovered? Then what were they supposed to do?

He sighed as he walked back into the bedroom to retrieve his bag. It was too early in the day for such painful topics. Once he got some strong hot coffee into his system, he'd feel more cheerful and less inclined to feel sorry for himself.

Asleep, Betty looked completely at peace with her world, as serene as a young child who still believed that real life offered the same happy endings as fairy tales. He wondered whether she'd wake up in such an untroubled state of mind, or whether she'd have her own uncertainties about their marriage.

A shaft of sunlight lit her hair, turning it from blond to gold. He bent to kiss her good-bye, then suddenly changed his mind, though he couldn't have said why, when they'd done so much more than kiss the night before.

He left the apartment with his duffel bag in one hand, his chocolate sampler in the other. He didn't bother to leave a note. If she wanted to talk to him, she knew how to find him through Mr. Sweeney.

The train to Sacramento was crowded, almost every seat taken by the time Paul got aboard. Either fewer cars were being put on the trains or more people were traveling than he recalled from before the war. He moved through the aisles, amazed by the numbers of travelers headed east across the state. Men, women, and children were all on the move. In pursuit of what? A new job? A nicer home? Greater opportunities? He wanted the same things they wanted. He just wasn't persuaded that Sweeney's Sweets was the most efficient route to achieve them.

The conductor was already calling "All aboard!" before he found what appeared to be the one available seat. In front of him a young woman was struggling to stow a very large suitcase in the overhead rack. He was about to offer to help her when the suitcase hit the edge of the rack, teetered in the air, and tumbled into the aisle. The suitcase hit the floor, the top sprang open, and a pile of women's clothing spilled at his feet.

He heard the young woman gasp in embarrassment as she whirled around and saw all the things that had fallen out. He opened his mouth to reassure her, no harm done, but one glimpse of her stricken face and the words stuck in his throat. She was beautiful, undoubtedly the most beautiful girl he'd ever seen. Her rich brown hair brushed against her cheeks like a velvet curtain, and her huge, liquid brown eyes were full of some dark emotion that he couldn't fathom. She looked like an exotic princess, royalty from a foreign country. For a crazy moment he felt as if he'd stepped out of time and space and been transported to a universe where nothing else existed but himself and this girl with the face of a movie star. She was a vision from the furthest recesses of his imagination, the girl of his dreams whom he knew could never be his. But for now, it was as if a magic spell had been cast around the two of them, a spell that he wanted to last forever.

He didn't want either of them to break the spell with speech, but then she said, "I'm sorry."

She looked as if she were on the verge of tears as she stooped to gather up her belongings. He couldn't bear to think that someone as exquisite as she was could be even the slightest bit upset. It went against all the laws of nature for her to be crying.

Dropping to his knees, he said, "Here, let me help."

She was holding a framed photograph of herself

in a graduation gown, standing next to an older man. The glass had shattered into a spiderweb of lines that crisscrossed the picture and made the man's face difficult to see.

"He's going to kill me," she said, her voice thick with fear.

From what little he could tell, the man in the picture, if that was whom she was talking about, didn't look crazy enough to murder someone because of a broken picture frame.

"It's just glass," he assured her. "You can replace it easy."

Clearly, he had said the wrong thing. Her bottom lip quivered, and he saw tears welling up in her eyes. He was about to apologize, though for what he wasn't sure, when the train lurched sharply and began to chug out of the station.

Caught by surprise, he lost his balance and was pitched forward against her, sending her sprawling into the middle of the aisle. Their tickets flew out of their hands as they landed on top of each other in a snarl of arms and legs, his face only inches from hers.

It was as if a current of electricity passed between them at the point at which their limbs met. He was stirred by an odd impulse: a yearning to reach over and touch her cheek, to see whether her skin felt as soft as he imagined it did. He saw that she was trembling, which gave him the crazy hope that she, too, had been affected by their accidental and oddly intimate collision.

They both scrambled to their feet, she blushing

bright red, he feeling clumsy and self-conscious, as if she could read in his eyes his longing to know her.

"Sorry," he said and realized that most of their conversation had consisted of one of them apologizing to the other.

"No, it's my fault. Oh, God," she said, her face crumpling. "Look at this mess." She gazed despairingly at her open suitcase, at the messy heap of clothes, her anguish seemingly out of proportion to the problem.

He bent over from the waist and scooped up their tickets.

"Here you go." He handed hers over with a grand, melodramatic gesture, bowing from the waist as the heroes always did in the silent movies.

He'd hoped to draw a smile out of her. Instead, she moaned, "Oh, no . . ." The color in her cheeks faded to chalky white, and her hand flew to her mouth.

"Are you all right?" A stupid question, if ever he'd asked one. Her ghostly pallor was evidence that she most definitely was not all right.

She shook her head. Her eyes darted left and right, like a trapped animal desperately seeking a path of escape. He took a step toward her, reaching out to comfort her, and saw that beads of sweat dotted her forehead. It occurred to him then that perhaps she was ill, that she might feel better if she were to sit down. But before he had a chance to make the suggestion, she gave a strangled, muted sob, opened her mouth, and proceeded to vomit up her guts all over the front of his uniform.

The passengers around them shrieked in disgust. The girl burst into tears, forced out an almost incoherent apology, and went running in the direction of the ladies' room. Paul stood frozen in place, momentarily too stunned to accept what had just taken place. The extremely vocal protests of his fellow travelers roused him from his shock.

He was tempted to go after the girl who was, after all, sick and maybe in need of help. But his shirt was soaked through with what looked to be the remnants of her breakfast, and the odor was as offensive to him as it was to the other passengers. His first order of business would have to be to clean himself up.

He hurried to the men's room at the other end of the car, apologizing all the way to the indignant people who held their noses as he passed, as if they'd just been sprayed by a skunk. He maneuvered himself and his duffel bag into the bathroom, which was thankfully vacant, and set about repairing the damage.

He peeled off the soiled shirt and rinsed it off as best he could in the sink. He had only one change of clothes in his bag, his rumpled salesman's suit, which he hadn't worn in four years. He pulled it out and somehow managed to get dressed in the confines of the tiny space. For the second time that day, he inspected himself in the mirror and was once again startled by his image.

His civilian self stared back at him . . . a slightly older, more mature version of the gung ho young man who'd been so eager to defend his country that he hadn't waited to be drafted. Both the shirt and jacket felt a little snug; he'd developed muscles from carrying his pack and rifle. The patterned tie seemed gaudy next to the unrelieved drab khaki of his uniform.

He removed the dirty shirt from the sink. The smell had faded only slightly, but unless he wanted to toss it away, there wasn't much more he could do until he got someplace with a washing machine. He was wringing out the excess water when he heard a loud knock and a voice demanding that he open the door.

The conductor glared at him. The look on his face silently accused Paul of attempting to cheat Northern Pacific out of its fare.

"Ticket, please," he said sternly.

Paul fished in his pocket for his wet, crumpled ticket. "Sorry. We had an accident."

The conductor grasped the stub with two fingers and punched the appropriate holes. "Yeah, so I see," he said, glancing disdainfully at Paul's soggy uniform before he moved on.

Paul stuffed the shirt into his bag, straightened his tie, and made his way back down the aisle, trying to ignore the unhappy passengers who crinkled their noses in disgust as he passed. The beautiful, sad girl had already returned. She was curled up in his seat, her head supported by the window, fast asleep.

Careful not to awaken her, he eased himself into the seat across the aisle and studied her face. Her lips twitched into a fleeting frown, and he hoped her dreams were free of whatever terrors she had been struggling with earlier. She was still pale, as if the blood had been drained out of her, and she looked exhausted by her recent ordeal. Even so, she had an air of grace and innocence, much like that of a picture of the Madonna he'd seen one time at an art museum.

Ignoring the view outside the window, he watched her as the train chugged east and north across San Francisco Bay, through Oakland, Lafayette, Walnut Creek, and Martinez. Finally, lulled by the monotonous rocking motion of the train, he drifted off into a nightmarish battle-scarred landscape. Bombs were dropping like hail from the storm-gray sky. Tanks spewed columns of fire. Wave after wave of troops had decimated the population, laid waste to crops and livestock, massacred every living thing. Tree branches, stripped bare by the fires, swayed in the wind.

His mission—the reason he'd been sent to this hell on earth—was to seek out and annihilate the enemy. Covered in soot, he crept through the fog, his flamethrower at the ready. A burned-out building loomed up at him through the gloom, a blackened shell with a gaping roof, broken windows, and a listing porch. He knew without reading the sign that lay on the ground that the building once had housed an orphanage. No longer, certainly; the children must be long gone, evacuated or dead. He'd yet to find a sign of life.

He was only a few feet away from the building when the door swung open. A woman stepped outside. Her face was hidden in the shadows, but he saw that she was almost naked, dressed only in a tattered slip. She was carrying something under her arm, and as she bent down to leave it on the porch, he saw that it was a baby's cradle, carved out of wood.

She straightened up and lifted her face to his view, and he realized that the woman was Betty. She looked alluring, sensual, vaguely dangerous. Then she was gone back inside the building, the door closed behind her. .

He moved closer, staying low to the ground until he reached the cradle. He pulled back the pale blue blanket that lay across the top. Instead of the baby he'd been expecting to see there, he found his unopened, unread letters. He knelt beside the cradle, about to scoop them up into his arms, when the wind suddenly picked up. The letters soared upward, many of them slapping him in the face.

He raised his hands to protect himself and woke up with a start, feeling unaccountably lost and scared. He couldn't immediately remember where he was. He blinked, and then it came back to him: Sacramento, the train, the beautiful girl . . . He turned to check if she was awake . . . she was gone! They were stopped at a station—Benicia, according to the sign. He craned his neck to see if he could spot her outside, but the platform was empty.

A pang of regret tugged at his heart. How sad to think he would never see her again. He didn't even know her name. An image of Betty in a torn slip came into his mind, and he realized he'd been dreaming about her, but the details had already gone fuzzy. Something about a cradle? An abandoned baby?

The conductor who'd earlier punched his ticket tapped him on the shoulder. "Your stop," he said.

The details faded to nothingness. He shook his head. "I'm going to Sacramento."

The conductor folded his hands across his potbelly and leaned close enough that Paul could smell the stale whiskey on his breath. "Mister," he said, "I've been punching tickets for thirty-two years next month on this line, and I ain't never misread a ticket, not once. And yours says Benicia."

His attitude reminded Paul of the much-despised bully of a drill sergeant who'd guided his unit through basic training. He couldn't wait to prove the conductor wrong. He pulled out his ticket and stuck it under his nose. "Here, look," he said. "Sacramen—"

He stopped, midword. There was no question about it. The ticket was stamped for Benicia. Flustered, he said, "I was sure—"

The whistle sounded, signaling that the train was about to depart the station.

The conductor smiled triumphantly. "Like I said, your stop."

Five minutes later, Paul was racing down the road, away from the train station to the Benicia bus depot. According to the stationmaster he had exactly one minute to catch the bus to Sacramento, and the next one after that wouldn't be leaving for three-and-a-half hours. He rounded the corner and saw that the bus was just pulling out of the depot.

"Hey!" he shouted. He waved his free arm frantically to get the driver's attention.

This sure as hell wasn't his day. Come to think of it, not a damn thing had gone the way it was supposed to from the moment he'd arrived in San Francisco. But maybe his luck would change, and the bus would stop, and he'd be spared wasting the next few hours watching the grass grow in Benicia.

The sun was glaring in his eyes, and sweat was pouring down his face. His chest was heaving like a bellows, but he kept on running. He'd put up with much worse in the army, daylong marches in the rain and snow with nothing to eat but a can of C-rations and a few swigs of tepid water out of his canteen.

"Hey!" he yelled again, narrowing the distance between himself and the back of the bus.

He kept on running even after he heard the brakes squeal and saw the bus roll to a halt.

The driver, a cheerful, overweight woman, grinned at him as she opened the door. "The speed you were going, you could have made Sacramento before me," she said and chuckled.

He was still gasping for breath, but he nodded his thanks as he climbed aboard and paid his fare.

The driver sniffed the air, and the smile on her face transformed itself into a grimace. She glowered at his bag, which had begun to emit a strong, distinctly unpleasant odor. "You smell anything?" she asked.

"No," he said as he hastily moved past her.

Every seat was taken at the front of the bus. Many of the passengers appeared to be migrant farm workers traveling north to Napa and Sonoma counties where the grape harvest would soon get underway. There were a couple of young men in uniform, and others dressed much like himself in business suits. He wondered whether they were also headed for Sacramento, and what kind of business they had there.

Betty had said that people were making lots of money, *hand over fist* was how she'd put it. He couldn't blame her for wanting him to ride that surge toward prosperity. She was probably thinking ahead to starting a family, and a baby couldn't be fed on dreams. Babies needed diapers and cradles and cribs. Suddenly, he saw a cradle full of letters, something to do with Betty . . .

An empty seat kept him from pursuing the image. He reached up to put away his duffel bag and was greeted by a sight that made him break into a smile. The battered suitcase belonging to the girl from the train was stowed in the luggage rack. The girl herself was sitting across the aisle from him. Her head was buried in a book, her face hidden behind her hair.

He leaned toward her and said, "Hi," as casually as he could manage.

She lifted her head. Her cheeks reddened with recognition.

He smiled, wondering whether his excitement showed.

She pushed her hair back and tucked a slip of paper into her book to mark her place. "Omigod, I'm so embarrassed," she said, her blush deepening.

He sat down, his heart thumping with the pleasure of seeing her again.

"I wanted to apologize," she said. "But you looked so peaceful."

"Apology accepted," he said.

She had a warm, wonderful smile and full, generous lips. He wanted to fly away with her to whatever magic kingdom she'd come from and live there with her forever. He wanted to know everything there was to know about her.

He could think of nothing else to say except, "Good book?"

She held it up for him to see the title: *Light and Dark Imagery in Shakespeare.*

"Quite a mouthful," he said, impressed that she was both smart and beautiful.

He'd always meant to read Shakespeare but hadn't gotten around to it yet. He resolved to buy himself a copy of *Romeo and Juliet* as soon as he got to Sacramento.

She shrugged and closed the book, which he took

as a positive sign that she was as interested in talking to him as he was to her. "It's required reading."

The only reading that he'd ever been required to do was the manual that George Sweeney handed out to all his new salesmen, the one that listed the top twenty guaranteed best sales techniques for placing chocolate orders.

"College?" he asked, feeling shy about his own lack of education.

"My master's degree."

He groaned inwardly. It wouldn't take more than a minute for her to figure out what an ignoramus he was. Sure, he loved to read. But he picked up novels mostly—Edna Ferber and Sinclair Lewis, Clarence Day and John Steinbeck—and he'd hardly cracked open a book while he was overseas. She was practically a professor. He couldn't have a conversation with her.

"Playing hookey?" he said finally. It was the best he could do, but he immediately wanted to kick himself for coming up with such a dumb comment.

She smiled wanly. "Going home. My family has a vineyard in Napa. We're always together for the harvest. It's our tradition."

He'd always wanted to visit the Napa Valley, which he'd been told was one of the most scenic regions in the state. He was fascinated by everything about her: the home in Napa, her matter-of-fact acceptance of family togetherness, the fact that she came from the kind of people who had created a tradition for themselves.

"Sounds like a nice one," he said, hoping his envy didn't show.

She sighed. "Yes," she said with a lack of enthusiasm that he found puzzling. "And you?"

"Business. In Sacramento."

"The train goes to Sacramento," she said, pointing out what he already knew.

"My ticket didn't." He smiled, feeling more philosophical about the mismarked ticket since it meant spending more time with her. "I mean, it did when I got on—"

"Oh, no." Her hands flew up to her mouth, and for a second he worried that she was about to be sick again. She reached into her bag. "I think this is yours." She handed him a train ticket. "I thought it was a mistake. I'm so sorry."

Her cheeks were the color of ripe cherries. He'd never met a girl who blushed as often or as gracefully.

The ticket was very clearly marked for Sacramento. So he had bought the right one, after all. He must have switched his for hers when he'd picked them off the floor of the train.

"As long as I get to Sacramento in time for the candy stores to open in the morning, I'm fine," he said.

"Is that your business? Candy?"

"Chocolate." He held up his sampler box and recited the company motto. " 'Sweeney's Sweets . . . can't be beat.' I'm a salesman."

"But wasn't that an army uniform I . . ." The color began to rise again in her cheeks.

He grinned and finished the sentence for her. "Decorated?" He nodded. "I was discharged yesterday."

"And you're back at work today?" She sounded impressed.

"You know what they say: 'Time is money.'"

Hearing himself, he frowned. The words sounded so foreign in his mouth. He didn't believe it for a moment.

Time was what you never had enough of; what you got to reclaim for your own when the army was through with you. Time was what was supposed to fly when you were having fun. But it had been such a long time since he'd had any of what he considered fun that he hardly remembered what it felt like. Fun was what he thought he'd have when he came back to Betty.

But Betty was the person who'd defined time as money.

"At least that's what my wife says," he glumly admitted to the girl.

She blinked hard, as if a loud noise had just erupted right in front of her—as if she were surprised to hear he had a wife. At that moment he wished more than anything that he was still a single man. But he was married, for better or for worse, and he owed it to this beautiful, sad, wonderful girl to tell her he was somebody's husband.

"She sounds very practical," she said.

He'd taken the train from San Francisco to Sacramento so often that he'd stopped noticing the scenery. But now, as he looked past her through the bus window, he felt a shift in his perspective.

"Practical's a good word. She has plans. For the future."

She held her hand against her stomach and said wistfully, "It must be wonderful to have someone like that in your life."

"Yes." Then why didn't he feel more appreciative? "And you?" He couldn't help it. He had to ask. "Do you have someone wonderful in your life?"

Tears sprang to her eyes, and a sob escaped from her throat.

"Are you all right?" he asked.

"I don't know what's wrong with me." She sniffled and attempted a weak smile. "I'm just so . . . sensitive lately." She took a handkerchief out of her bag and dabbed at her eyes. "I'm not usually like this."

"Well, look on the bright side. You'll be home soon with your family."

His attempt to console her triggered a fresh flood of tears. She began to weep as if her heart were broken.

"I'm sorry." She wept and turned away from him, her shoulders shaking with suppressed sobs.

Her grief felt so sharp and deep. Perhaps someone she loved had recently died . . . a brother or boyfriend, killed in battle. But that didn't explain her earlier outburst on the train when the picture had broken and she'd cried over the man she thought was going to kill her.

She was like a character out of a movie, dark and mysterious and possibly in danger. He wished he could do something to make her feel better. But he didn't have any idea what sort of trouble she was in, and he didn't know how to ask. Hell, he didn't even know her name.

CHAPTER

· 3 ·

The bus bounced along the rutted one-lane road past gently rolling pastures dotted with ponds that sparkled in the late afternoon sun. Herds of dairy cattle grazed lazily amidst the fat bales of hay that would provide their feed through the winter. Men on horseback turned to stare as the bus passed by, churning gravel. Their dogs barked a sharp warning that was audible even above the roar of the engine: Keep out. No strangers welcome here.

Every few miles the road was intersected by a muddy path cut wide enough for a tractor to pass. In the distance, at the end of the path, Paul occasionally spotted a farmhouse with children playing in front. Once, he caught sight of a woman hanging sheets on a clothesline; he thought he saw her pause to wave at the bus but couldn't be sure. A band of boys loped by carrying fishing rods over their shoulders. They were laughing and chewing gum as they strolled down the road, and they looked so carefree that he wished he could jump off the bus and join them.

Though the windows were open as far as they could go, the faint breeze provided little relief from the stifling air. He caught himself nodding but fought his drowsiness because he wanted to stay awake in case the girl wanted to talk. Eventually, despite his best intentions, the heat overpowered him and he dozed off into a restless sleep.

He jerked awake when the bus stopped in what appeared to be the middle of nowhere to pick up a couple of passengers. He glanced quickly across the aisle and was relieved to see the girl was still on the bus. She was staring out the window, her book lying unread on her lap.

He felt stiff and thirsty and wished he had a bottle of soda pop to wash away the dust in his throat. He glanced at his watch and saw that it would be another couple of hours before they reached Sacramento. He wondered when the girl would be getting off the bus and whether she'd tell him anything more about herself before she said good-bye.

The two new passengers lumbered down the aisle, leering at the women as they walked by. Paul idly watched their progress. He'd met lots of men like them in the army, obnoxious louts whose greatest talents lay in picking fights and making trouble. These two looked like farmers, but he knew plenty of men who'd been raised in big cities who were just as rude and ignorant.

His eyes were flickering shut, but he snapped to

attention when one of the men stopped in front of the girl.

"This seat taken?" he asked her. He winked broadly at his friend.

She looked up at him, shook her head no, then went back to staring out the window.

The man lowered himself into the seat next to her, while his friend took a seat just behind him and leaned over to watch the fun.

The man tapped the girl on the arm. "So, how ya' doin?" he said.

When he got no response, he turned and smirked at his friend. Then he twisted around so that his face was just inches away from the girl's.

"I'm Bill," he said, still smirking. "And this is my buddy, Herman. And you're . . . ?"

The girl inched closer to the window. "Not interested," she said, barely glancing at him.

Bill hooted with laughter. "I had a girlfriend once. Always used to say she wasn't interested. But that ain't what she ever meant." He jabbed his friend in the ribs. "Was it, Herm?"

Herman chuckled in agreement. "Most definitely not."

"Not when she got to know me," Bill loudly declared. He moved closer to the girl and draped his arm over the seat so that it almost came to rest on her shoulder.

"Stop it!" she said. She sat up very straight to avoid his touch.

Encouraged by Herman's laughter, Bill again

shifted his body toward hers. "Oh, c'mon. Just give it a shot."

Paul had hoped the men would lose interest quickly and leave the girl alone, but now he saw that they were just getting warmed up to their game.

"Fellas," he said in a quiet but forceful tone, "the lady doesn't want to be bothered."

Bill spun around and thrust his finger under Paul's nose. "Hey!" he growled. "You value your health, you'll keep your nose out of my conversation, shithole."

A rush of adrenaline surged through him, but he didn't flinch. Bill was a bully, obviously looking for a fight. He was full of bluster, but at heart he was a coward who was begging to be taught a lesson in how to read a lady. Paul was ready to teach him that lesson. As a kid he'd been skinny and defenseless, a natural target for the bigger boys who'd used him as a punching bag. The army had toughened him up, preparing him for hand-to-hand combat against an enemy far more formidable than Bill could ever dream of being.

Though he preferred a peaceful end to the confrontation, he was prepared to take on both Bill and his buddy if he had to. "Just let her be," he said, his voice still calm and controlled.

Bill's face had turned crimson with anger. A vein was pulsing in the middle of his forehead as he stood up and reached over with the clear intent of grabbing Paul by the front of his shirt.

He didn't even get close. Paul blasted out of his

seat like a hand grenade, bringing to bear all his training as a seasoned combat soldier. He hurled himself at Bill, grabbed his arm, and pinned it behind his back. Bill yowled in pain and struggled to break free of Paul's hold, but Paul was too strong for him.

A split second later, Herman was on his feet, rushing at Paul with clenched fists. Paul stepped back and Herman lost his balance, which gave Paul all the advantage he needed. He grabbed the back of Bill's neck and slammed his head forward. His aim was deadly accurate. Bill's forehead smashed into the bridge of Herman's nose. Paul heard a loud crack, and the men howled in unison. Paul dropped his hold on Bill, who cradled his head in his hands, while Herman bent over, his palm cupped against his broken, bleeding nose.

The bus screeched to a halt. The driver stood up, her hands on her hips, and let it be known that nobody was going anywhere until all three trouble-makers hauled their asses off her bus. The girl tried to explain that Paul was a hero, but the driver wasn't interested. She had a route to run, a schedule to keep. She didn't tolerate fighting, drinking, or cussing. And she definitely didn't want to be mopping blood off the floor. She wanted them out, she reiterated. To make sure her point was made, she marched down the aisle, grabbed Paul's bag, and tossed it into the road.

Bill and Herman put up a token resistance to save face. But they'd been whipped, and they knew from the angry expressions of the other passengers that they had little choice but to leave, or risk another beating. Paul reluctantly trailed them down the steps, all the while pleading his case for justice with the driver. He was only defending the lady—behaving as a gentleman was supposed to—maintaining order and safety on the bus.

The driver glared at him from her seat and shook her head. Star salesman though he was for Sweeney's Sweets, she wasn't buying any of what he was selling this afternoon.

"But I have to get to Sacramento," he said, throwing himself at her mercy.

"Not on this bus you don't," the driver declared. She slammed the door shut in his face.

The bus rolled away, spewing pebbles and dirt as it hit the road. Through a cloud of dust, he caught a glimpse of the girl, gazing at him forlornly through the rear window. He stared after her, his stomach churning with frustration and anger.

During the heat of battle, with bullets flying in every direction and men who were his friends dying alongside him, he had developed a strong belief in the power of fate. His philosophy for staying alive had evolved from one principal tenet: If destiny decreed that his name be inscribed on one of those bullets, so be it. The best he could do for himself was to keep his rifle clean, keep his head down, and pray.

Now, it seemed that fate was amusing itself at his expense. How else could he explain the way he kept meeting up with—and being separated from—

the sad, beautiful Madonna? It was almost as if the gods were mocking him for wanting too much, taunting him with a vision of what could never be his.

He kicked at the dirt, conscious that Bill and Herman were standing just a few feet away, apparently contemplating their next move. They sauntered toward him, and he scowled, a warning that there was more to come of what he'd given them if they ventured any closer. Sufficiently admonished, they froze in their tracks. He picked up his duffel bag and started down the road, fairly certain that he'd seen the last of their ugly faces.

The sun was beginning to dip down beyond the horizon, but the temperature had cooled by only a few degrees. With no choice but to walk, he trudged along, tired, thirsty, and discouraged. Another bus would pass by in a few hours, but it would be dark by then, and the driver could easily miss seeing him. He suddenly recalled a favorite saying that his sergeant had repeated often, claiming that Mark Twain had originated the thought: No good deed goes unpunished. There was no doubt about it, though he couldn't imagine having done anything else under the circumstances.

The road stretched ahead with nothing but pasture and trees on either side, the only visible landmark the foothills of the Mayacamas Range rising to the east. The nearest town might be miles away, and the chances of his getting to Sacramento by nightfall were dimming as quickly as the setting sun. The early evening sky was already deepening from pink to violet, and the only sounds he heard were the birds twittering in the branches and the occasional, far-away lowing of the cattle.

He marched on, trying to draw some pleasure from the beauty of his surroundings. But it was not until he rounded a curve in the road that he unexpectedly came upon a sight that truly lifted his spirits. Just a few yards ahead, a woman sat hunched with her back to him on her battered suitcase. Even from behind, he recognized her from the fall of velvety dark hair around her face.

His footsteps caught her attention. She looked up as he approached. Her eyes were rimmed with red from crying.

He had already made up his mind. Even if he never saw her again after tonight, he had to know her name.

If she hadn't been feeling so utterly wretched, Victoria almost might have smiled at the handsome young man who kept reappearing when she least expected him. She couldn't imagine what he must think of her. She'd brought him nothing but trouble, and she could never repay him. But now at least she could properly thank him for all his kindnesses, especially the way he'd bravely rushed to rescue her from those two horrible men on the bus.

Another few minutes and she would have missed him. Normally, she would already be halfway up the hill to the house. She was so tired, though, that she'd stopped to rest by the road, a chance to think about the ordeal that lay ahead of her. Part of her had wanted to stay on the bus until the last stop, wherever that was. She could choose a new name, begin a new life for herself, disappear so completely that her father would never find her.

As tempting as the fantasy was, she could never fulfill it. She could never stop being Victoria Aragon. No matter what happened, she could never run away. Her connection to her family went as deep as the grape rootstock her great-grandfather had planted in the mid-nineteenth century. She didn't agree with her father's old-fashioned beliefs, but she loved him very much.

As a child, she'd basked in his love. She couldn't count the number of times she'd hurried home from school to tell him that she'd gotten the highest mark on a test, written the best essay, been named the class valedictorian. He'd been so proud of all her accomplishments. But on the day she ran to find him in the vineyards because she'd received the long-awaited letter accepting her to college in San Francisco, they'd had their first terrible fight.

They'd never fought about her going out with boys. She was too shy and studious to care much about dating. Besides, the boys she went to school with from the valley were like her brothers. It was fun to ride horses and swim and dance with them, but she certainly had no interest in kissing any of them. She was saving her kisses for her *caballero,* who was waiting for her somewhere beyond the Napa Valley.

Her father, however, had other plans for her. He didn't want her to go to college. He wanted her to stay at home, like a proper Mexican girl, to learn to cook and sew and take care of a house—to prepare to be a good wife to the man whom he'd already handpicked for her to marry.

She didn't eat for a week after he told her about the arranged marriage. She lay down on her bed and announced to her worried mother and grandmother that she would rather die than give up her college education. She may have been descended from Mexican aristocracy, but she was a born and bred American girl. She wasn't about to be handed over to the son of one of her father's friends like some prize heifer at the country agricultural fair.

Her father should trust her to behave herself away from home, she declared. Then she turned her face to the wall, away from the windows that looked out onto the vineyards, and waited for his answer.

Of course, he'd let her go, though he'd never quite forgiven her for defying him. And he'd let her go again when she'd announced her intention to continue on for her master's degree. Part of him wanted his children to have the education they deserved. But part of him also wanted her to obey him absolutely and unequivocally.

Tom had once remarked that she had fallen in love with him precisely because it was so very much the wrong thing for her to do. She hadn't understood what he meant, and she'd sworn to him that he was mistaken. She'd been waiting all her life to meet him, she'd said.

Now, sitting by the side of the road, she was beginning to grasp the truth in his comment. How pleased he would have been to hear her admit he was right. The mistake had been hers. To believe in his love. To believe that he could be trusted.

She dried her eyes and tried to compose herself as the young man from the train caught up with her.

"I don't think we've been properly introduced," he said with a smile. "I'm Paul Sutton."

"Victoria Aragon," she said as he sat down next to her. "I'm sorry about the bus. I feel terrible . . . all the problems I've caused you. You should just keep going. Who knows what will happen to you next?"

She tried to smile, to show that she was making a joke. But there was too much truth behind her question, and her lips quivered as she swallowed her sobs.

His smile seemed genuine, as if, despite all she'd done to him, he was happy to see her again. "There's always the possibility of an earthquake, I suppose. Why aren't you on the bus?"

"This is my stop."

"Are you waiting for a ride?"

She shook her head. "No." And then she began to cry again, thinking about what lay in store for her on the other side of the hill. Her father's fury would descend on her like a storm at sea, annihilating whatever lay in its path. "He's going to kill me," she whispered, imagining his rage.

"Who?" Paul asked.

She didn't want to burden him any further with her problems, but he was so kind and gentle that she couldn't help herself. "My father," she said, weeping.

"Listen, if you're still worried about that picture frame, the nearest hardware store should have—"

"It's not about the picture," she broke in, still weeping. "Oh, God!"

The enormity of what she'd done grabbed her by the throat like a crazed dog. She should never have come home. She may as well have thrown herself off the bridge and spared her father from turning into a murderer.

"It's none of my business," he said hesitantly. "But if you'd like to talk about it . . ."

Though normally she would have cut out her tongue before she'd share such an intimate piece of her life with a stranger, the temptation to tell him was too strong to resist. She felt as if she'd known Paul Sutton forever. She could trust him with her shameful secret. She reached into her pocket for the letter Tom had left her and handed it to him.

Hearing him read it aloud, she flinched. Nevertheless, she let him continue. She needed to hear the words spoken, in order to make them become more real.

"'I was not meant for the conventions of this world, not meant to be tied down. I am a free spirit. . . .'" He looked at her, puzzled. "Who's a free spirit?"

"*Light and Dark Imagery in Shakespeare.*"

He shook his head, still not understanding.

"My professor," she choked out between sobs. "He and I were . . . we were . . ."

She couldn't bring herself to finish the sentence. Whatever words she used would make what had happened between Tom and herself sound so tawdry and cheap. But it hadn't been at all like that. The love they had shared had felt pure and romantic. They'd recited Shakespeare to each other by candle-light, read poetry together in bed, discussed great literature as they walked by the bay.

She forced herself to meet Paul's eyes. What must he think of her now? That she was no better than a whore? And he didn't even know the worst of it yet! In San Francisco the fact that they weren't yet married had seemed such a minor detail. She knew they'd be married eventually. In the meantime, "*Carpe diem,*" Tom always used to say. Seize the moment.

"Well," he said slowly. "I don't know your father, but I don't think that just because some 'free spirit' broke up with you . . ."

No. She didn't want his kindness. It hurt too much, because it was so undeserved.

"I'm pregnant!" she whispered. She dropped her gaze. The closer she got to home, the more keenly she felt her shame.

His long stunned silence didn't make her feel any

better. She could sense him floundering to find the appropriate reaction. The wedding ring on his finger was proof enough of what he must feel.

She raised her head and through her tears stared at the purple-shaded mountains where she'd learned to ride. They were so much a part of her existence that she'd never noticed them until she'd come back for the harvest the first year she'd gone away to college. Then she'd seen for the first time how they rose above the valley like a fortress, insulating the vineyards and the families who planted the grapes from the world beyond.

Perhaps her father had been correct to not want her to venture beyond those mountains. How different things would be if she'd stayed here, safe and protected from temptation. But she was the great-great-granddaughter of the man who'd crossed the mountains and sailed across the ocean. Exploring the New World was in her blood.

Adventures were often undertaken at a cost. Now she would have to pay for hers with her life. She didn't even try to stop the tears from flowing as she started to get up to walk the rest of the way home.

Paul carefully folded up the letter and handed it back to her. "You're very upset," he said. "I can understand that. But look at the positive side. It's a new life coming into the world. And your family . . . they seem very close. I mean, harvesting together and all that."

" 'I will kill anyone who dishonors my family!' "

she hissed at him. "How many times has he said that? A hundred times? A million times?"

"I'm sure it's just a figure of speech."

"It's not!" she insisted. "My father means what he says. Always. He's very old-fashioned. If I come home this way, without a husband, he'll kill me. I know he will!"

She slumped back onto her suitcase, drained and defeated by the mere idea of confessing to her father.

The air around them was still except for her muffled sobs, the quiet so intense that she jumped when Paul snapped his fingers.

"How about if you do show up with a husband?" he asked.

But she'd already told him . . . she didn't *have* a husband.

"A friend who can pretend," he explained, looking pleased with himself for having figured out a solution.

The idea was so sweet and silly it almost made her smile. But it could never work. "They know all my friends, especially the boys. I was brought up very strictly."

He pondered the problem, then said, "Well, how about someone from the city?"

She shook her head. That went beyond silly to just plain dumb. "Who does what? Comes for the day? And then just leaves?"

"Sure." He squinted into the fading light as he slowly wove together the details of the story. "He comes to meet the family, stays one night, leaves in the morning, puts a letter in the mailbox on the way out saying he's . . ."

"Abandoned me?" She frowned, playing the scene out in her imagination.

He nodded. "And the baby." He punched the side of his duffel bag. "The rat! It happens."

Something in his voice—a roughness she hadn't noticed before—made her wonder whether he actually knew a man who had abandoned his wife and baby. A rat. A man like Tom. Still, his idea was so far-fetched. "This is silly," she said.

"What's the worst your father can accuse you of? Bad judgment?"

"They'd never believe I could just marry somebody out of the blue."

"Why not? It happened all the time during the war. People would meet, get married, sometimes before they even knew each other's last names."

Once again, he seemed to be speaking from his own personal experience. That possibility saddened her.

"You're very kind to try to help me. Maybe it would work. But there's nobody . . . and I have to go." She picked up her suitcase, sighing deeply as she turned to leave. "Thank you again for all your help."

She couldn't have gotten more than ten yards down the road when she heard him calling her name. "Miss Aragon . . . Victoria . . ."

She turned around. He was waving at her, walking quickly in her direction. She stopped and waited, noticing that he'd put on his hat, as if he were going to make a formal call. While she waited for him to catch up with her, she thought about how different her life would be if she'd met a man like him instead of Tom.

When he caught up with her, he tipped his hat to her and grinned. "There's me," he said.

CHAPTER

· 4 ·

Paul insisted on trading his sample case for her suitcase, and as they trudged together up the incline, Victoria realized she never could have managed the suitcase on her own. As often as she'd walked this path, it had never seemed so steep or long. She guessed it was the pregnancy that made her feel exhausted to her core. It was as if heavy weights were tied to her arms and legs, so that walking became an effort, and carrying anything heavy was out of the question. She would have had to leave the suitcase behind, to be fetched later by one of the men, which would have given her father more reason to be annoyed with her.

She should have called ahead to say she was coming, to have someone meet her bus. But she'd been anxious to get away from San Francisco as quickly as possible, before she lost her nerve and went running to find Tom instead of coming home.

She'd also been afraid that, hearing her family's voices, she might break down on the phone and confess the whole sordid tale without properly preparing them.

If only she could get to her mother first, speak to her alone, beg her to make her father understand. She still remembered, as if it had happened just the week before, how Beata Velasquez, the older sister of one of her friends, had mysteriously been sent in disgrace to live with her aunt and uncle in Los Angeles.

"She's better off dead," Alberto Aragon had declared. But Victoria's mother had wept in sympathy for the poor girl and her family, and hugged Victoria tightly, as if to ward off the possibility of such a thing ever befalling her.

Even then, only ten years old, Victoria had suspected that whatever Beata's crime, she didn't deserve to be exiled so far from home. Her papa was wrong and her mama was right, she'd confided to her dolls, who were as curious as she was about the nature of Beata's naughtiness. By the time she pieced together enough information to satisfy her curiosity, her dolls had long since been stored in the attic for her own daughters to play with, and Beata was married to a wealthy LA gringo. Her son resembled neither her nor her husband, but nobody seemed to care anymore, least of all Beata's parents, who proudly showed off their grandson to everyone in the valley.

So such stories could have a happy ending, Victoria consoled herself—especially if she and Paul were able to give a convincing enough performance that her father was persuaded they were husband and wife. Certainly, he would still be furious with her for marrying a man about whom he knew nothing other than his name and the fact that he was a candy salesman. And his suspicions about her poor choice would only be confirmed when Paul "abandoned" her. There was bound to be gossip about her in the valley. But at least her baby would never be called a bastard, and she might be spared the full force of her father's wrath.

She looked sideways at Paul, who was bent almost double under the combined weight of the two bags and hadn't uttered a word since they'd started walking. "If you're having second thoughts or anything like that, I understand," she said, suddenly stricken with the fear that he'd changed his mind.

"Let me explain something about myself," he said, almost stumbling over a rock. "Ever since I was a kid, my word's my word. Do or die. Hold on a sec. I need to catch my breath." He stopped short, panting, and unceremoniously dropped the two bags onto the ground.

"Was it horrible? Being in battle?" she said, too shy to ask him the personal questions that really interested her.

He stretched his arms over his head, working the muscles in his shoulders. Then he said, "Before was horrible. Once the shooting starts you just go blank. But before . . . the trick was to get your mind on something else. Some guys would sleep. Some would sing every song they knew over and over. . . ."

He looked away from her and fell quiet, as if he were listening for the sound of those songs.

She pictured him in a foxhole somewhere in France or Italy, his rifle pointed at the unseen enemy, trying not to focus on the coming storm of bullets and blood and death.

"What did you do?" she asked.

"I wrote letters to my wife in my head." He bent down to tie his shoelace and closed his fist around a handful of pebbles. "Then later . . . after . . . I would write them down. One time we were stuck in this trench for like thirty hours . . . I wrote a fifteen-pager."

He pulled his arm back, warming up like a pitcher at the mound, and tossed the pebbles, one by one, into the tall grass on the side of the path.

"About the war?"

"About what I'd like our life to be like when I got home. The perfect little house, the kids running around in the yard with the dog, the great job."

His description exactly fitted her image of his life. It included everything that she wanted for herself and that Tom had most disdained. "The bourgeois dream," he'd labeled her vision of their future together.

The first time he'd used the word, she'd nodded, as if she'd understood, and looked it up later in the dictionary. It was French, meaning middle-class, and therefore conventional or smug. Tom was a self-proclaimed rebel; a Bohemian, he'd called himself. She'd thought she could change him.

"You described your life for fifteen pages?" she asked, jealous of the woman fortunate enough to receive such a letter.

"No. That was just the first two pages."

"And the other thirteen?"

"I just went on and on about how much I loved her."

He shrugged, as if embarrassed to continue. She nodded encouragement, her eyes telling him she wanted to hear everything.

"How when I got home I just wanted to hold her, gaze in her eyes from sunrise to sunset, forever and always. You know, stuff like that. It's not poetry, but—" He shrugged.

"Yes, it is," she broke in, touched by his honesty. "She must have cherished every word."

"Yeah, every word," he said curtly.

His wife had somehow disappointed him. She could hear the hurt in his voice, and she wondered what his wife had done to upset him. Perhaps he'd asked her to keep the letters for him to read and she'd thrown them away by mistake. There was so much more she wanted to know about him, whether he'd had the kind of homecoming he'd described, whether he'd found the house with the yard yet.

It was just her bad luck that she'd met Tom instead of someone like Paul Sutton, who was so good and decent and wanted all the same things she wanted. All it had taken was one encouraging look from Tom, and she'd been smitten.

He *was* a rat, and a liar, too, swearing that his love for her would last until the end of time. It hadn't even lasted until the end of September! And all those awful poems he'd written about her, the ones that began, "To Victoria, by moonlight," and "Thou art more beautiful than the sun. . . ." She'd written better poetry than that when she was in high school. The pity was that she'd believed his lies and made such an idiot of herself.

"You're very kind to do this for me," she said, watching Paul struggle with their bags.

"And the baby. I'm doing it for both of you."

"Then we both thank you," she said and smiled for the first time since she'd read Tom's letter.

He returned the smile, and her heart did a funny little dance in her chest. She hung back for a moment, not wanting him to see how moved she was by his goodness. She could easily love a man like Paul Sutton. But he was married, and she was pregnant, and there was nothing for her to do now but pray that her father wouldn't see through the flimsy fabric of their deception.

Paul gasped with pleasure when he reached the crest of the hill and discovered the heart of the Napa Valley nestled below him, spread out like a magnificent Persian tapestry. Following the contours of the terraced hills, dappled golden and red by the setting sun, was an endless sea of lush vines, heavy with their bounty of bursting purple grapes. The vineyard stretched as far as he could see; it was interrupted only by a cluster of buildings dominated by a Spanish-style hacienda in front of which towered an enormous oak tree.

The air was softly scented with the perfume of the grapes, intoxicating his senses. He felt as if he were perched on the edge of paradise; he couldn't imagine that any evil, unkind word could ever be allowed to disturb the idyllic peace of the valley.

He stood mute, content to drink in the view, awed by the splendor of the setting. He wanted to memorize the vista, to remember that such extraordinary places existed in the world. He came from farm country that was flat, dull, monotonous. The Napa landscape could inspire poetry in the soul of a candy salesman.

Victoria came to stand by his side. "We call it *Las Nubes*," she said softly. "In Spanish it means the clouds."

"It's beautiful," he said, seized by a desire to put his arms around her. Her lips would feel so soft. Her breath would smell like the air, rich and grapey. He sighed, knowing he could never fulfill his desire.

"Yes," she said sadly, and he allowed himself to imagine that she shared his desire.

The spell of the moment had been broken. It was time to breach the walls of the castle and defend the honor of his princess. In the few fairy tales he'd read as a boy, the villain was usually the wicked stepmother. Victoria hadn't mentioned any step-mother. But from her description, her father sounded sufficiently frightening to play the role of the villainous king who wanted to cut off his daughter's head because she'd kissed the frog and he hadn't turned into a prince.

He turned and stared at her, to fix in his mind the idea of her as his wife. Betty's face flashed in front of him, and he heard her reciting Armisted Knox's ridiculous sentences, imitating his phoney, affected accent. Four years was a long time to be separated from someone you loved. She'd changed so much, she hardly resembled the girl he'd left behind. He wondered if she thought the same about him.

He remembered how she'd looked on their wedding day, so pretty in the new dress she'd bought especially for the ceremony at City Hall. Afterward, they'd ridden the cable car to Chinatown for lunch, and Betty had hardly eaten a bite of her chop suey because she'd been so busy admiring her brand-new wedding ring. She'd given him one, too. All the modern couples were having double ring ceremonies, she'd said.

Which reminded him that Victoria was missing something important if she was properly going to play his wife. Fortunately, he had just the thing to complete the picture of them as a happily married couple.

"If we're going to do this right . . ." he said. He opened his sampler box and took out a piece of chocolate that was wrapped with a thick gold foil band. "The Wedding Bon Bon Deluxe. A big seller around June."

He smiled as he slipped it onto her slender ring finger. Her cheeks were colored pink from blushing. He imagined himself down on his knees, asking her to marry him. He imagined her saying yes, she'd be pleased to be his wife. He felt drunk with the romance of the moment . . . the setting sun, the perfumed air, the beautiful princess Victoria. . . .

The crack of shotgun fire shattered his reverie. His battle-honed survival instincts kicked in. He dove for cover and hit the ground with his hands folded over his head.

A second blast, this one closer than the first, reverberated through the stillness. He glanced up and saw Victoria, still standing, totally exposed to the maniac who was ripping up the countryside with his bullets. He sprang into a half crouch, grabbed her by the waist, and dragged her down beneath the shelter of the nearest grapevine.

He lay on top of her, his ears alert to the direction of the incoming fire. She struggled to free herself, and he put his finger to his lips to warn her to be quiet. Victoria's eyes were round as two saucers, mirroring his alarm.

Silence—the kind of eerie silence that experience had taught him not to trust. Then he heard what he'd been waiting for. The rhythmic slap of a man's footsteps along the path, a man who was so sure he'd cornered his prey that he didn't care if he signaled his approach.

Paul peered first right, then left, trying to plot an escape route. Behind them was the open, unprotected dirt road. In front of them, the path curved steeply downward toward the vineyard. The footsteps got louder, closer. His bare hands were his only weapon, scant competition for a man with a shotgun. If it came down to it, he could take on the shooter while Victoria ran for safety.

He tensed his body like a coil, poised for attach.

A pair of boot-clad feet appeared in front of him. The barrel of a shotgun pointed not six inches away from his face.

The trick was to play for time.

"We're unarmed. Don't shoot," Paul said as calmly and forcefully as he could manage.

He pushed himself to his knees, raised his hands in the air, and stood up very slowly and deliberately, so as not to startle his assailant. Face-to-face, he saw a man in his late forties, with fiery dark eyes set above a prominent nose and a thick, well-groomed mustache. He was carrying a shotgun in one hand, a brace of freshly killed pheasant in the other.

Before he could stop her, Victoria scrambled to her feet and brushed the dirt off the front of her dress. "Hello, Papa," she said nervously.

"Victoria?" The man's mouth turned downward in a suspicious frown as he glanced from his daughter to the stranger with his hands stuck over his head.

"Who is this?" he demanded, speaking with a heavy accent.

Her voice was shaking as she made the introductions. "Alberto Aragon, my father. Paul Sutton, my husband."

Her eyes were glued to the ground, as if they were weighted down by her lies.

Paul lowered his arms and extended his hand to shake Alberto's. "Glad to meet you, sir," he said.

Alberto glared icily at Paul as he raised the shotgun until it was pointed directly at Paul's chest. Paul held his breath and said his prayers. Victoria had said her father would kill her for dishonoring the family name. Now, he finally understood why she'd taken the threat so seriously.

After what seemed like hours but couldn't have been more than a minute, Alberto lowered the gun. He spat on the ground, as if to express his scorn for his new son-in-law. Then, with a jerk of his thumb, he motioned for them to follow him back to the house.

Not a word was spoken as they marched down the hill and along the path that intersected the vineyard. Victoria felt as if a cold wind of fear had lodged itself in her body, causing her to tremble so violently that she could hardly hold on to the Sweeney's sampler. Her only comfort came from feeling Paul's sturdy presence alongside her. She didn't dare speak to him, or even look at him, for fear her father might take aim at Paul with the same deadly accuracy he'd used on the pheasants.

She clutched the sampler case against her breasts and mentally replayed the sound of Paul's heart hammering in her ears when he'd thrown himself across her body. She'd been fairly certain that they weren't in any danger, that the shots were probably being fired by her father or grandfather who often hunted small game in the hills. But she'd felt Paul's willingness to sacrifice his life for hers and got caught up in the drama of the moment: the damsel in distress saved by her knight in shining armor, like Sir Gawain of King Arthur's Round Table, whose tale she'd studied in her medieval literature class.

Now, however, images of English literary heroes had been replaced with the much more vivid image of the bloodied pheasants swinging by their necks over her father's shoulder. Her stomach was going funny again, the queasiness growing worse as she watched the pheasants sway from side to side across her father's broad back. She couldn't bear to look at them, yet she couldn't seem to tear her gaze away from the awful sight of their tongues lolling between their beaks. She swallowed hard, trying not to see the drops of blood trailing from their wounds as a terrible omen of things to come.

"Marie Jose!" Alberto shouted, not breaking his stride for an instant as he stomped into the house.

Victoria cast a despairing glance at Paul.

"It'll be okay," he quietly reassured her.

Not quietly enough, however, because Alberto instantly whirled around and brandished the rifle barrel at him.

"Like hell it will be okay!" he roared. "I will not allow this! I'll go to the pope himself to get this undone!"

"We weren't married in a church," Victoria whispered nervously.

Her comment only exacerbated Alberto's rage. His deep-set eyes bulged with fury, and for one horrible moment, he looked ready to pounce at the couple with his bare hands.

"Marie Jose!!" he bellowed. His voice bounced off the low stone ceiling of the hacienda and echoed through the hallway that led to the inner rooms.

"*Que pasa, Alberto?*" Marie Jose Aragon came bustling out of the kitchen, wiping her hands on her apron.

She was an older version of her daughter, with flashing brown eyes and the graceful bearing of a woman who'd been brought up in elegance and comfort. Still beautiful at forty-two, she was possessed with a warmth that didn't need words to express itself.

"*Cual es el problema?*" she said. She spoke calmly, as if she took for granted her husband's tantrums. And then, catching sight of her daughter, she threw out her arms. "Victoria!"

Victoria ran sobbing into her mother's embrace. She buried her head on her shoulder, finding there the comfort she'd yearned for from the second she'd discovered Tom's letter on the mantel.

"Here is the problem!" Alberto glared at his wife, as if she were somehow to blame. He pointed his shotgun at Paul, who gingerly pushed the barrel toward the floor.

"Is this how you were brought up?" Alberto

shouted at Victoria. "To betray your mother and father?"

Victoria clung to her mother like a little girl hiding behind her mother's skirt. "I did not betray anyone," she timidly defended herself.

"What on earth are you talking about?" Marie Jose demanded of Alberto. Gently, she pushed her daughter away and peered into her face. Victoria once again burst into tears and fell back against her mother's shoulder.

"The gringo! I'm talking about the gringo!"

Victoria flinched at her father's disparaging designation of the man she'd introduced as her husband. Yes, Paul was an American, but so was she, and only someone as closed-minded as her father would deem his lack of Mexican ancestry tantamount to a criminal offense. "His name is Paul, Papa!" she boldly declared.

Before Alberto had a chance to respond, Guadalupe Aragon came into the hall to investigate the source of the commotion.

"*Hijita, linda!*" she cried, full of joy at the sight of her beloved granddaughter.

"*Abuelita!*" Victoria hugged her grandmother, who was the seventy-three-year-old matriarch of the family, a pure-blooded Mexican Indian who could trace her lineage back four thousand years.

Before she could open her mouth to introduce Paul, her father began to lecture Marie Jose about Victoria's conduct. "A girl's place is here, at home, not alone in some city doing God knows what!" he thundered.

The line was an old, familiar one that the family had heard often in the days before Victoria had staged her hunger strike and received Alberto's permission to go to college. Marie Jose and Guadalupe exchanged bewildered glances. They'd thought that issue was dead and buried. Why bring it up now, in front of a stranger, a guest in their home?

"I'm going to school there! That's what I'm doing!" Victoria cried, shamed by the knowledge that she'd fulfilled her father's worst fantasies. She folded her hands across her belly, unconsciously shielding her unborn baby from Alberto's anger. He'd already veered so close to the truth. She wasn't yet ready to admit that she was pregnant.

"Will someone please tell me what's going on?" Marie Jose repeated with a hint of exasperation.

"Your daughter is married!" Alberto's tone of voice was a mixture of horror and recrimination. He'd expected the worst, and Victoria had more than fulfilled his direst predictions. Somebody had to be held responsible, and the two best candidates—his wife and his mother—were standing right in front of him.

Marie Jose was too stunned to say a word, but Guadalupe instantly filled the gap. "*Felicidades, querida!*" she said, congratulating Victoria with a heartfelt kiss on the cheek.

"Mama!" Alberto loudly objected to his mother's enthusiastic response.

Anger. Love. Resentment. Shock. Fear. Joy.

The various members of the Aragon family were slinging emotion-laden arrows at one another so quickly and with such intensity that Paul could hardly keep track of what was happening. It was as if he'd been catapulted into the middle of a thick stew of feelings, which seemed to have nothing and yet everything to do with his presence there.

He had kept silent, having decided that this was strictly a family matter, though he was, after all, supposed to be Victoria's husband. Perhaps they were waiting for him to speak up on her behalf. But he felt lost and out of place among them, an intruder who didn't speak their language, even when they stuck to English.

He was still trying to decide what his role should be when an older man, who also appeared to be in his seventies, white-haired and powerfully built, wandered into the house, dressed in overalls and muddy boots, as if he'd just come from the vineyard.

"Grandpa!" Victoria ran to him and folded herself into his embrace. "Make him stop! Please!"

Victoria's grandfather raised a bushy eyebrow at Guadalupe, who shrugged her shoulders. She was almost as mystified as he.

Alberto glared first at his wife, then at his mother and father in turn. "That's right, coddle her! The whole bunch of you!" he burst out angrily. "But I'll tell you right now, this will not stand so long as I draw breath." He raised his right hand, as if taking an oath, and thundered, "I swear before God!"

"Alberto!" cried his wife, shocked by his vehemence.

A torrent of barely suppressed tears broke through Victoria's wavering dam of self-control. "You are so unfair!" she screamed. Then she bolted out of the room without even a backward look at Paul. Marie Jose and Guadalupe hurried after her, leaving him alone with Victoria's father and grandfather.

Alberto scowled at Don Pedro. "Me?" he raged. "I'm unfair? *I* came home to tell my family that I spit on their trust?" He jabbed his finger into his own chest, scoring each of his points." *I'm* the one who came home to rub in their face that I married this . . . this . . ."

He spun around and glowered at Paul. "What *do* you do?"

Paul instantly decided that the only way to make Alberto believe the big lie about his being Victoria's husband would be to tell the truth about everything else. He held up his Sweeney's sampler. "Chocolate," he said. "I sell chocolate."

Alberto stared at him as if he'd admitted to being a convicted murderer. "No," he said, sounding stricken.

Confused by Alberto's reaction, Paul nodded, yes, he was. To prove his point, he opened the sampler case and showed Alberto the neatly laid out rows of individually wrapped chocolates.

Alberto shook his head disbelievingly and turned to Don Pedro. "You're the head of the family," he blustered. "Say something!"

Paul braced himself for the worst as Don Pedro, a formidable figure who radiated a quiet strength and dignity, walked over and scrutinized the box of chocolates. Then his unflinching gaze moved away from the chocolates and met Paul's uncertain eyes. He held out his right hand and said, "I am Pedro Aragon. Welcome to our family."

Don Pedro's show of support momentarily jarred Paul. He'd expected more shouting, accusations, a military-style interrogation as to his intentions and prospects. He felt deeply grateful to Don Pedro for the kindness, for the hope that he'd be Victoria's ally in the battle she had still to fight with her father.

"Thank you," he said, clasping Don Pedro's callused, well-muscled hand.

"May I?" Don Pedro pointed to the box of chocolates.

"Uh, sure," he said, again caught by surprise. "Help yourself."

Don Pedro smiled happily as he gave the contents of the sampler case careful consideration. He reached for his selection, hesitated, came close to choosing a second chocolate, changed his mind again, then finally picked out the most gaudily wrapped piece in the box, a cherry-centered dark chocolate. He quickly dispensed with the wrapping and popped the piece in his mouth, savoring the flavor with obvious relish.

Paul didn't know what to make of his performance. He was relieved, of course, but also confused by Don Pedro's disregard of his son's wrath.

Alberto, on the other hand, was very clear in his feelings about Don Pedro's gracious acceptance of the stranger his daughter had brought into their midst. He wanted nothing to do with him or his damn chocolates or his father's show of hospitality. His daughter had betrayed him, his mother and wife had defied him, and his father had insulted him. Incensed beyond words, he stormed out of the house and slammed the door behind him, leaving Paul and Don Pedro to get acquainted all on their own.

CHAPTER

· 5 ·

Marie Jose and Guadalupe indulged Victoria in a good, long weep, holding her hands and fussing over her as if she were still a small child. They brought her a wet cloth to fold over her swollen eyes and glass of cool well water to soothe her raw throat. As she wept, they spoke to her about the grapes, the goings-on among the other wine-growing families, their hopes for the harvest. Neither of them said even one word about Paul, the marriage, Alberto's reaction. There was plenty of time to talk, but first she had to rest and calm herself.

Nothing good ever came of trying to converse with someone who was tired or hungry or upset. This line of philosophy, originated by Guadalupe and handed down by her to Marie Jose, was the secret of their successful coexistence with Alberto. He was not an easy man, Guadalupe had often admitted to Marie Jose during the early, somewhat difficult days of her marriage. He felt things strongly and was inclined to react without thinking. But he was honest and good and loving, if one handled him properly. Victoria, however, had yet to absorb the lesson, in spite of their repeated efforts to teach it to her.

Soothed by their ministrations, she eventually stopped crying and became aware of the delicious aromas wafting up from the kitchen. It was almost time for dinner. Unlike some of the other valley women, Guadalupe and Marie Jose didn't feel that they'd grown too rich or sophisticated to keep their hand in the cooking. In their minds, feeding their family was an act of love, and their love showed in the food they prepared. Thus, even on this occasion, with Victoria a sobbing newlywed and Alberto sulking in his office and a stranger for a son-in-law, they had a meal to put on the table.

Maria and Consuela, the two women who helped with the cooking and cleaning, were already in the kitchen, chopping and peeling and stirring. The other women joined them and began preparing the sumptuous dishes that were typical Aragon fare. The family grew or hunted most of its food. Tonight, as usual, there was an abundance of choice: freshly killed pheasants; avocadoes, tomatoes, green beans, pumpkin, and potatoes; rice and tortillas.

The kitchen, with its arched windows and brightly tiled walls, had always been one of Victoria's favorite rooms. It was a place for laughter and gossip and telling stories, with space enough for more than a few cooks. In the middle of the kitchen was the square wooden table where as a child, she had spent countless late afternoon hours, peeling potatoes and chopping onions.

Now she sat down, leaned her elbows on the top, and set to work scraping the potatoes. She became absorbed for a time in removing every inch of peel as smoothly as possible, just as her grandmother had taught her. But her resentment toward her father was smoldering beneath the surface.

When a potato skidded out of her hands and shot across the table, it was all the excuse she needed to throw down the paring knife and demand of her mother, "Why can he never just say 'I'm happy for you, Victoria. Congratulations, Victoria.'? Why must everything be a drama?"

"It is a bit of a shock," Marie Jose said, grinding fresh pepper over the tortillas.

"Not for Grandma or Grandpa. Not for you. Why is he always this way?" She slammed the paring knife onto the table. "I hate him!"

"Victoria, he's your father," Marie Jose said sternly.

"He has never taken change well," Guadalupe diplomatically intervened. "Even as a child, he was this way. Only with the vines he has patience." She sighed as she picked up a mixing bowl, perhaps wishing she'd raised him to be otherwise.

Victoria angrily pursed her lips. How often did she have to hear her father's bad temper excused for lack of patience? "Well, maybe he should have some for us, too. That would be nice for a change, don't you think?"

"You could have at least prepared us," Marie Jose gently chided her daughter. "A call. A letter. That would have been wiser, no?"

Yes. Of course, her mother was absolutely right. If only she could have prepared them. If only . . . She picked up the knife and became very involved in peeling another potato. "I wanted to surprise you."

"Well, you certainly succeeded," said Marie Jose.

"He wants me to marry some man in Mexico I have never even met. Just because he has the right bloodlines. I am not a horse, Mama! It's my choice who I marry. Not his!"

Guadalupe glanced over at Consuela and Maria, who had stopped what they were doing to listen to the conversation. *"Muchachas, la comida,"* she said, her quiet tone belying the authority of her command. The meal needed to be prepared, no matter what crisis the family was preoccupied with.

Victoria pushed back her chair and walked over to the window. To the right of the kitchen door her mother had planted an herb garden with rosemary, basil, thyme, and dill. Beyond the garden was a brick pathway that led to a shallow pond, bordered on one side by a crescent-shaped trellis where brilliant yellow roses bloomed in the early summer. Alberto had built the trellis himself and planted the roses as a gift for his young bride, and Victoria had always imagined that her wedding would take place right there, on the gentle rise that overlooked the vines.

Now she would never have her romantic wedding, the strolling musicians, dancing and wine and good food.

A bouquet of herbed scents floated up to her as she leaned out the open window. She sighed and turned back to her mother. "How many times have you told me, 'The heart wants what the heart wants?'" she said, still imagining the storybook wedding she would never have.

"And this is what your heart wants?" her mother asked.

"Yes." So she'd thought then. Now she'd have to live with the consequences.

Marie Jose fixed her with a long, penetrating gaze. "Really and truly?"

"Really and truly." She nodded her head vigorously, trying to look the picture of a radiant young bride.

Marie Jose's eyes were like two searchlights, probing for the truth, penetrating the hidden recesses of Victoria's soul.

She had never lied to her mother. She'd never had reason to lie before today. The deception was like a thick veil that hung between them, distorting her vision and muffling her true voice. She wanted to push the veil aside and tell her mother her secrets. But the truth felt too dangerous. So she pressed her lips together to keep herself from speaking and made her eyes go blank as she raised them to meet Marie Jose's.

"All right," Marie Jose said finally. She put her

arms around Victoria and hugged her tightly, not seeing the tears of anguish that splashed across her daughter's face. "Everything will be fine," she promised. "You will see. Everything will be perfect."

Left to his own devices while dinner was being prepared, Paul had wandered through the rows of carefully manicured vines, inhaling the heady mix of the rich loamy soil and the ripe, soon-to-be-picked grapes. A man could fall in love with this country, he thought, staring up at the omnipresent mountains silhouetted against the dusky sky, where a moon that was just short of full was rising to the west. Exploring further, he passed a cluster of vine-covered buildings, a grove of cypress trees, a large uncovered barrel lying on its side, waiting to be repaired.

He picked a grape and crushed it between his thumb and forefinger. The stain of its skin looked like blood and tasted like sugar. What was Betty doing tonight? he wondered as he turned and retraced his steps. Was she playing her Armisted Knox record and reading about how to get ahead in the world? He kicked at a pebble, playing it with his shoe as if it were a football, noticing the erratic pattern of light and dark filtering through the windows of the hacienda. Shadows of leafy branches danced against the white stucco facade, graceful ghosts in the darkness.

The scene he'd witnessed earlier between Victoria and her family had left him feeling shaken and confused. The whole idea of family was very mysterious to him, especially one as noisy and warm and unpredictable as the Aragons seemed to be. Though he didn't regret what he'd offered to do for Victoria, he wished he had a guidebook to steer him through the twists and turns that lay ahead in the next few hours. He didn't belong here at *Las Nubes*, any more than he belonged with someone like Victoria. Alberto had recognized that immediately. He hoped her mother and grandparents were less astute and more forgiving.

The need for a guidebook became even more pressing when he joined Victoria and her family in the elegant, high-ceilinged dining room. The table was formally set with delicate white china, two sets of sparkling crystal glasses—one for wine, one for water—and gleaming silverware that felt heavy in his hand. Two women, wearing long white aprons and caps, stood against one wall, awaiting the signal to begin serving.

Alberto had changed from his work clothes into a tie and jacket. He sat silent and unyielding, like a volcano waiting to erupt. Paul was seated next to Victoria, who inexplicably looked even paler and more frightened than before. He wanted to reach over and take her hand and whisper in her ear not to worry. But he thought better of it when he saw Alberto glaring at him from the head of the table.

Marie Jose came in, smoothing her bun and smiling as she sat down across from them. No one said a word. The tension was as palpable as if it were an actual living presence that had joined them at the table and was filling the room with its foul-odored toxic fumes.

Paul sipped his water and nervously cleared his throat. He was about to say something—about the weather, the grapes, anything to break the silence—when Guadalupe appeared on Don Pedro's arm. Like Marie Jose, she had discarded her apron and changed into a simple but flattering dress. She, too, smiled at Paul. Then she kissed Victoria on the forehead and waited for Don Pedro to pull out her chair before she sat down next to her granddaughter.

And still, Alberto mutely glared at Paul, as if daring him to further intrude upon the sanctity of their family circle. The women's hands fluttered nervously, adjusting the white linen napkins folded next to their plates, straightening the already perfectly aligned silverware. Only Don Pedro seemed impervious to the chilly atmosphere in the room.

"Such a delicate ring," he said, coming around to the other side of the table and gallantly kissing Victoria's left hand. "You look beautiful tonight. Marriage agrees with you, no?"

As he took his seat, he surveyed the abundant array of serving dishes that Maria and Consuela had brought to the table. He smiled approvingly and nodded at Guadalupe, signaling her to say grace.

Paul did as the others, folding his hands and bowing his head as Guadalupe recited, "Bless this food we are about to eat. And bless the harvest of the grapes You have given us in Your wisdom and grace. Amen."

"*Bon appetit,*" Don Pedro declared, reaching for the dish that was closest to him.

The others followed his lead and helped themselves. All the while, the two servants hovered in the background, waiting to refill an empty platter or to fetch whatever was missing.

"This is made with pipian . . . pumpkin seeds," Victoria told Paul, serving him tortillas, rice, and a generous portion of mixed steamed vegetables. "It's a specialty of my grandmother's."

He'd thought he'd be too nervous to eat, but the food was so tempting that after one taste he was immediately hungry for more. "It's delicious," he said, checking to see whether he was using the right fork.

Alberto paused midbite and frowned. "It's been in the family cookbook since before the Declaration of Independence was signed," he declared belligerently, making it sound as if Paul had insulted Guadalupe's culinary skills.

"So," Marie Jose quickly interjected, "with all the commotion, we never heard the whole story of how you two met."

Paul and Victoria glanced at each other. They'd never discussed the details of their romance. He didn't even know how far along she was in her pregnancy. Certainly, that wasn't a subject he ever would have broached, but now he counted the months backward as he scrambled to think of an answer to Marie Jose's question.

"I was on leave in June—" he began.

"July," Victoria cut in. "Just after I moved to the city."

He restrained himself from looking to see Alberto's reaction. "Oh, that's right, July." But where would a soldier meet a girl like Victoria? He thought of Betty, of how they'd met. "At the USO," he added.

Marie Jose nodded at Consuela to refill her husband's wineglass. "I didn't know you worked at the USO," she said.

Victoria tugged at her hair. He sensed that she was trying to think of an answer that would satisfy Alberto. "I wasn't actually working there."

Alberto slammed down his knife. "Then what were you doing in a hall filled with strange men?" he growled.

Paul frantically cast about for a plausible explanation that he could offer on Victoria's behalf. That she'd gone to a dance there would obviously not pass muster. A poetry reading? Too implausible. Whoever heard of a room full of GI's showing up to listen to poetry? A dance performance? He doubted that Alberto would approve of his daughter up on stage, showing her legs off to the troops.

"Don Pedro," Guadalupe said gently, inadvertently providing a diversion. She shook her head in disapproval as she caught her husband in the act of sprinkling his food with a liberal helping of salt.

"*Mi abuelo vivio*," Don Pedro said, turning to

Paul. Then he caught himself and switched to English. "Excuse me, my grandfather, he lived to one hundred and two. Used salt like he was a fish in the sea. My great-grandfather, one hundred and six, also . . ." He mimed throwing a handful of salt onto his plate and sneaked a look at Guadalupe. She smiled adoringly at her husband. Don Pedro winked at Paul and firmly set the shaker down on the table.

Alberto wasted no time resuming his cross-examination. "So tell us, Mr. Sutton," he said sarcastically. "Since we now have such a clear picture of how you two met, where are you from?"

"Moline. Moline, Illinois."

"Wherever that is." Alberto sneered.

"It's in the middle of the country." Victoria rushed to defend the honor of Paul's birthplace. "Exactly in the middle. Right?"

Paul nodded. "Right."

"And your parents?" asked Marie Jose. "They're still in Moline?"

"I never knew my parents," he said.

"Then who brought you up?" Alberto taunted him. "The fairies?"

His cruel gibe hit Paul in his most sensitive spot, the place deep inside where the pain of his upbringing had yet to heal. "I grew up in a home," he said softly.

"Whose *home*?"

The eating had stopped. Even Don Pedro had put down his fork and knife to follow the volley of acid-dipped questions flying across the candlelit table.

"An orphanage," he said, trying to hide the hurt that swam to the surface whenever he was forced to talk about his past.

Seasoned hunter that he was, Alberto sniffed out a wounded animal and moved in for the kill. "Wonderful. This is just wonderful." He railed at Paul. "My daughter can trace her ancestors back four hundred years to some of the finest families in Mexico, and you are telling me she has married a man with no past." He hooted derisively. "Worse . . . a man with no past *and* no future."

All the years of discipline and obeying orders had left their mark. Paul had been well taught to respect authority, bite his tongue, respect his elders. There was much he wanted and could have said to Alberto, but his training wouldn't permit the words to flow. Alberto was Victoria's father. His host. He had to honor him by keeping quiet even if he didn't respect him.

Victoria, however, had no such qualms. However afraid she may have been of her father, she couldn't allow him to viciously insult Paul. To his surprise, as much as her own, she burst out, "You don't know that he has no future. You don't know anything about him."

"Do you?" Alberto challenged her.

She hesitated a moment. Alberto leaned forward on his elbows and rubbed his hands, sure that he'd trapped her.

But she fooled him—and Paul, as well. "Yes. I know he knows how to love somebody. How to appreciate them." She smiled at Paul and went on. "I know he wants a house with kids running around with the dog in the front yard. I know he wants a great job."

He'd thought she was just being polite, asking him all those questions. But she'd actually cared enough to listen and remember. It moved him greatly that she'd come to his defense.

"You mean like the one he has?" Alberto snapped.

Guadalupe tsked her disapproval, and Marie Jose frowned at her husband, but no one said a word. The two servant women stood stiff and impassive. A gust of cool wind fluttered the curtains of the open windows. The candles flickered for an instant, and then their flames grew steady again.

Paul thought about the long rectangular tables where he'd eaten all his meals at the orphanage, where a boy's palm could get a sharp strapping if he broke the rule of silence at the table. He remembered the total absence of kindness shown by any member of the staff, the way he'd been made to feel as if it were his fault for having been deserted by his father and abandoned by his mother to the care of others.

He'd tried so hard to be a good boy, always nurturing the hope that some day he'd be chosen from among all the others by a childless couple in search of a son whom they could lavish with love and toys. He'd created in his imagination the house they'd take him home to, the bedroom he'd have all to himself, the brand-new puppy they'd buy him as a gift to celebrate his arrival. And at dinnertime, they'd all three of them sit around the cozy dining room table, and he'd be allowed to talk as much as he wanted about all the wonderful things he'd done that day, and chocolate cake would always be served for dessert.

Even after he was old enough to understand that nobody wanted a boy—even a smart, well-behaved one—of fourteen or fifteen or sixteen, he still clung to the image of his perfect, loving parents in their perfect, snug little house. At night, in the dormitory room he shared with nine other boys, he'd fall asleep thinking about the bedroom he'd never have, the one with all the balls and books and games picked out specially for him. Or he'd think about how eagerly his perfect parents would listen to all his stories, while his mother passed him a second helping of the chocolate cake she'd baked that day because it was his favorite.

Perhaps those perfect parents didn't exist outside of his imagination. Perhaps even in real families, fathers were as strict and even cruel sometimes as the matrons who'd set the rules at the orphanage. Or maybe they just did what they thought was right for their children, though their behavior might seem harsh and difficult. It was too much of a puzzle to piece together all at once, but one thing he knew after four years of hard combat. He didn't have to stick around to be a verbal punching bag. Not for anyone. Not even for Alberto Aragon.

"Excuse me," he said, getting up from the table. Mindful as always of his manners, he turned to

Guadalupe and smiled. "It was very good. Thank you."

He left the dining room without another word and went outside to fill his lungs with the clean, fresh country air.

The ink-black sky was a brilliant silken canvas painted with a million glittering stars, the Milky Way a luminous splash of pale white ribbon arching across the face of the night. Force of habit required Paul to locate the North Star glowing at the tip of the Little Dipper, the bright anchor by which explorers from ancient times to the present had oriented themselves. At almost full moon revealed the outlines of the surrounding mountains, hulking dark shapes that needed the light of day to show their true form. From somewhere in the hills a coyote howled plaintively. His cry was answered by a series of raucous yelps that echoed across the profound stillness of the valley.

The door creaked open as Victoria came out onto the porch. She came to stand so close to him he could almost feel the brush of her sleeve against his arm. He felt her shiver as she stared up at the sky. Though the air felt balmy on his face, she folded her arms across her chest, as if she were cold.

He studied her profile and said, "He doesn't pull any punches, does he?"

"I'm sorry," she said without looking at him. "You must think they're horrible."

He searched for a way to explain what he felt. "When I was a kid, every night at the orphanage," he said finally, "I'd climb up to the roof and make a wish on every star I could see."

He saw her smile. "That's a lot of wishing."

"Well, it usually boiled down to one wish, really."

She turned to look at him, her eyes wide and curious, inviting him to share his secrets, assuring him she could be trusted not to laugh at or betray his answer. "What was that?"

A thought streaked across his mind like a shooting star. She would have read his letters, each and every page of them. "For what you have in there," he said.

"A bunch of people always telling you how you should live your life?" She raised her chin and made a noise with her lips, *phht,* to express her disbelief.

"Better than having no one telling you," he said softly, remembering how it had felt when he'd realized that nobody cared what he did with his life as long as he obeyed the rules: made his bed in the morning, took a bath once a week, said please and thank you, ma'am to the orphanage superintendent, and didn't get into fights with the other boys.

"I don't know about that."

"I do."

"That's still no reason for him to treat you that way," she said angrily. She pushed her hair away from her face, and he found her even more beautiful now than he had before.

"No." He agreed with her. "And I was going to

say something. But then I thought, what if it were me. A strange man comes into my house, tells me he's married my daughter, and I'm the last to know. I'd probably act the same way."

"No, you wouldn't." She frowned, as if annoyed that he would even suggest such a possibility.

"I don't know about that," he said.

"I do."

He'd never met anyone else like her—so fierce and certain in her opinions; at once brave and resolute, frightened and timid. She'd inherited her mother's grace and beauty, but she'd also inherited a good deal more of Alberto's nature than she would probably care to admit.

Lamplight suddenly blazed through the window behind them, shone across her face, then was just as suddenly extinguished. In that brief moment he found in her eyes a reflection of his own inner turmoil. He was married; she was carrying another man's child. Yet what he was experiencing with her went far beyond friendship, into a realm where he'd never before ventured. His feelings for Betty had been simpler and much more easily categorized. The emotions flowing now between Victoria and himself were like the ocean, vast and deep, powerful and potentially very dangerous.

The air around them felt heavy and charged with electricity, as before a lightning storm, though there wasn't a cloud in the sky and the wind was calm. Paul's hand was trembling with the need to touch her. Instead, he forced himself to glance at his watch.

"It's only another eight hours and I'll be back on the road," he said. "I think the worst part is over, don't you?"

Victoria smiled weakly. The coyote howled again, and Paul heard sadness and longing in his cry. He waited for its mate to respond, but this time no answering call came echoing through the night.

"This bed was part of my dowry when I married Mr. Aragon," Marie Jose told Paul as she moved from corner to corner, deftly tucking the sheets under the mattress.

Paul and Victoria stood watching her from the doorway of the master bedroom, the room she shared with Alberto, who was nowhere to be seen. The bed was large and imposing, with an elaborately curlicued antique brass headboard and footboard. Marie Jose had changed the sheets herself, replacing the old ones with a clean set and a freshly laundered, snowy white duvet cover.

"It was my grandmother's before that," she went on, plumping the down comforter. "Her dowry . . . she brought it all the way from Paris. He was a diplomat, my grandfather. It's where we spent our first wedding nights . . . my mother, my grandmother, me."

She straightened up and inspected her handiwork, checking for wrinkles or lumps. A quick adjustment to the comforter, a shake of a pillow, and she was satisfied.

She smiled at Victoria, who squirmed with embarrassment under her gaze. "We can sleep in Pedro's room," she said.

"It's bad luck for newlyweds to sleep in separate beds. Besides, your brother comes home tomorrow."

"Then we'll sleep in my room."

"In that little teeny, tiny bed?" Marie Jose threw up her hands in mock horror. "For your wedding night? No. You need room . . . to maneuver. . . ." She winked broadly at Paul, who shifted from leg to leg, wishing he could think of any good excuse why he should sleep in the guest room.

"Mommy!" Victoria blushed.

Marie Jose pushed the window open another inch and fiddled with the shade.

"I know this is not your first night, but I would like to think it is," she said. "It's just that from the first night all our marriages have been blessed. Call it superstition. I just want you to have what we have. . . ."

The words failed her as she gazed adoringly at her firstborn child, her beloved, only daughter. A few tears fell as she hugged Victoria, then turned and embraced Paul.

"It is out of love my husband roars so. We are very traditional people, Paul," she haltingly explained. "Sometimes the modern world takes a little getting used to. He will come around."

Earlier, she'd brought up a vase of red roses and

set it on the table next to the bed. They hadn't fully bloomed yet; the petals were still folded inward around the center, delicately perfumed layers of softness. Marie Jose removed one from the bouquet and placed it in the middle of the long round pillow that lay the length of the bed. She stood a moment, her hands clasped behind her back, and looked from bed to Victoria and Paul.

There were tears in her eyes, but she was smiling as she gave them her blessing. "Love each other always," she said.

CHAPTER

· 6 ·

"Alberto!" Marie Jose crooked a finger at her husband, who had come upstairs and was heading toward his bedroom. "Alberto!" she whispered again and waved him into Victoria's bedroom.

It was still very much the room of a young girl, filled with mementos of her childhood: fuzzy stuffed animals, some with the fabric worn thin from love; Victoria's horse show ribbons; all the awards she'd won in high school for good citizenship and academic achievement; her books and pictures. And her narrow, single bed.

One glance at the closed door of his room—at his nightclothes laid out across the chair, at Marie Jose already dressed for sleep in her nightgown—and he immediately understood what his wife was up to. "No!" he protested.

Marie Jose nodded yes. She drew him into the room and shut the door.

His wife was a wonderful woman, but sometimes she could act *loca* . . . crazy. Already this evening he'd been subjected to a scolding from his mother—as if he were the one acting like a small child!—for being rude to their guest—his daughter's husband.

The very words galled him. Watching Victoria run from the table after Paul Sutton, his gut had contracted with anger. Nevertheless, he'd finished his dinner, if only to prove to his wife and mother that his life would go on as usual, in spite of the gringo.

He paced the room, fuming at Marie Jose. "First he comes into my house and steals my daughter. And now he takes my bed? No!" He marched toward the door. "No!"

Marie Jose got there first, blocking his exit. "*Querido*," she said, her voice a caress. "You don't want to see it, but your daughter is a woman. And she was not stolen any more than you stole me. Have you forgotten?" she asked, touching his lips in the special way he loved. "The little room under the stairs in my father's house?"

She ran her hand across his chest. He smiled in spite of himself. He recognized the look in her eyes, a remembrance of long-ago passion that still burned like the heat of the August.

They'd met when she was seventeen and just finished her schooling at a Paris convent. He'd come to Mexico on a visit and was staying with an uncle who was a friend of Marie Jose's parents. He was twenty-four, the only son of a respected winery family—a man with prospects, with a future.

Theirs hadn't been an arranged marriage, but it well could have been, so delighted were both families with the match. It was hard to say who had wooed whom, for despite her convent education and demure smile, Marie Jose had very clearly conveyed her desire to be Alberto's wife.

"I asked for your hand properly. With respect. Who is he? He is nobody!" he said, his anger wavering as he responded to her touch.

She rubbed her face against his cheek like a cat and said softly, "He is her choice. And she is our daughter. It is from us she has learned how to be who she is. If we don't have confidence in her, then how can we have confidence in ourselves?"

Her logic defied argument. Her hands and mouth were an invitation to pleasure he could never refuse. He undid the top button of her nightgown and kissed the hollow at the base of her neck.

As his fingers moved down to the next button, she stopped with her hand. "First go and wish them a good night," she murmured. "So they will not go to bed thinking you are furious with them."

"But I *am* furious with them!" he said, smiling as he stroked her hair.

"You should smile more. You are so handsome when you smile," she said softly.

She touched his face with her fingertips, lingering on his lips. He moved closer, but she shook her head, no, not yet. She sealed her promise of what was soon to come with her moist mouth. Then she opened the door and stepped aside so he could go make peace with his daughter.

After much protesting by Victoria, they had finally worked it out that she would sleep alone in her parents' bed, and Paul would sleep on the floor in a makeshift bedroll. Paul had assured her that during the war he'd slept for weeks and months at a stint in far worse accommodations, which only made her feel more guilty about his having to spend yet another night on a cold, hard surface.

She stared at the blanket, sheet, and pillow they'd spread on the floor as she took the pins out of her hair and began to brush it, as she did each night before she went to sleep. Except last night, she realized, her hand frozen in midair. Was it only twenty-four hours since she'd come home to her empty apartment and found Tom's note?

It felt as if she'd lived a lifetime since then, in which she'd changed from a little girl to a woman, stood up to her father, and met the kindest, most wonderful man in the world. The man who was now perched on the edge of the bed, writing the letter that would implicate him as an irresponsible scoundrel.

She fought the urge to throw down her brush, run across the hall to her parents, and shout, "You don't understand! Paul's not the one to blame. He was only trying to help me out!" But if the thought of Paul Sutton as their son-in-law was hard for them to get used to, the truth would be impossible for them to accept. For the rest of her life she would have to live with her lies and the fact that a man she'd just happened to meet on a train had been willing to do so much for someone he hardly knew.

She sighed as she began to get undressed. As if to reassure her, he said, "Once your family reads this you'll be in the clear. My name will be mud, but what the heck?"

She stared at the back of his neck, which looked so exposed because of his short army cut. "Do you like selling chocolates?" she asked him, her voice muffled as she pulled her dress over her head.

He put down his pen and was quiet for a moment. "No. Not really."

"Why are you doing it?" she asked, struck by what she heard as doubt in his voice.

"That's part of what I thought I would use this trip for . . . to try and figure things out for myself."

She shook her head as she folded back the bed covers. "But you have things figured out. The house . . . the kids . . . the dog. That sounds pretty figured out."

"It's not that easy," he said, staring into the blackness of the night. "There's more to it. It's . . . complicated."

She picked up the rose that her mother had laid on the pillow and thought about her dream of carrying a bridal bouquet of yellow roses. "It doesn't sound that complicated to me."

He was quiet for so long that she wondered

whether she'd somehow offended him. "You're not married," he said at last.

The unintentional cruelty of his comment hit her with the force of a well-aimed punch in the stomach. Try as she might to stop herself, she couldn't keep from crying out in pain.

He instantly realized the damage he'd done and turned around to apologize. "I didn't mean . . ."

She saw him drinking in the sight of her in her white slip that clung to every curve and contour of her body. Almost against her will, she grabbed her robe and held it against herself.

"It's just not a good time for me now," she said tearfully, clutching at the robe as if it were a life preserver. "You've been wonderful. More than wonderful." He couldn't seem to tear his eyes away from her, until finally she said, "Would you turn around, please?"

He nodded guiltily and did as she'd asked. "There'll be someone for you," he said.

She slipped into bed and covered herself with the sheet. "You don't have to make me feel better."

"No, I believe that. I believe that there's a perfect someone for everyone. Someone who will love you, no matter what." He bent his head again to the pad of paper, shook his head, threw down the pen, and went to stand by the window. "I mean, who knows?" he said, his back still to her. "Tomorrow you could turn the corner and meet that one guy who falls madly in love with you . . . thinks you're the most beautiful woman. The most perfect woman. Who wants you and the baby so badly . . ."

His fantasy of her future sounded so sweet, so full of wonderful possibilities, that she ached to believe him. He sounded so convincing, as if he could actually see that one guy walking down the road, headed in her direction. She closed her eyes and tried to see him, too. But the only face she could conjure up was Paul's, and though he was smiling at her, he wasn't alone, because just behind him, hidden in the shadows, was his wife.

She opened her eyes and looked around the pretty room where her parents had spent their entire married life. There were pictures of the family on the walls, fresh flowers on her mother's dressing table, her father's comb and brush laid out on the top of his dresser. Her grandmother had hand-embroidered the pillow on the rocking chair, and her grandfather had built the huge oak wardrobe where her mother kept her dresses and shoes.

She hadn't slept in her parents' bed since she was a little girl, sick with fever, and her mother had let her nap there as a special treat. Their bed had seemed huge compared to her own child's bed, yet she'd felt so snug and peaceful tucked in among the pillows that smelled of rose petals and grapes. She'd always imagined that one day she would share just such a bed with her husband, the mysterious *caballero* of her dreams, the man Paul was describing. But his fantasy was just that. A fantasy. A fairy tale that no longer had anything to do with her life.

"Would you marry someone if it wasn't your baby she was carrying?" she asked.

He turned around to look at her. "If I loved her," he said unhesitatingly.

There was something in his expression she couldn't read . . . or didn't want to. She was tired, she told herself. Overwhelmed with all the conflicting emotions of being pregnant and coming home and losing Tom. She made her mind go blank and reached over to turn off the lamp. "Good night," she said.

"Good night," he answered her.

She could hear him taking off his clothes and trying to make himself comfortable on the floor, which creaked as he turned from side to side. She was beyond exhausted, beyond fatigue, yet she knew sleep wouldn't come. Not with him lying only feet away from her, a narrow, yellow beam of moonlight streaming across him like a beacon.

He sighed, and so did she. She cleared her throat, and he coughed. She rolled over onto her stomach and hit the pillows.

There was a sudden, sharp knock at the door, then her father's voice. "May I?"

"One moment, Papa!" she called as she bolted upright and frantically signaled Paul to come lie next to her.

One swift kick sent his sheet flying under the bed. He leaped under the covers with her just as Alberto opened the door.

"Your mother sent me to wish you good night," he said curtly.

The light from the hall illuminated his face. His eyes were narrow slits of coal, his mouth a curved sword waiting to be unsheathed. His voice was as unyielding as the mountains. But he was there, even if it was at her mother's insistence.

"Good night, Papa," she said.

"Good night, Mr. Aragon," Paul echoed.

A gust of wind pushed the door open another inch, and the shaft of light from the hall widened. It caught the gleam of white sheet peaking out from under the bed, and the pillow that lay on the floor beside it.

She saw her father take note of both, then glance suspiciously at her. She held her breath, but he didn't come any farther into the room to investigate.

"Good night," he said.

The door closed behind him with a firm click.

She and Paul waited one, two, three beats, until they heard Alberto walk into Victoria's room and shut the door. As if on cue, they turned to face each other, their bodies so close that she could feel the heat radiating off his chest. Her heart was pounding beneath the thin fabric of her nightgown. She was sure he could hear it, just as clearly as she could hear his labored breathing.

Their hands lay on the pillow, just inches apart. If either one of them stirred, there'd be no way to stop their falling into each other's arms. She closed her eyes, which made the longing worse. When she opened them, he was staring at her unblinkingly.

"Does the door have a lock?" he whispered.

"No."

He had thick, curly lashes that slanted down at the outer corners of his eyes. In the pale light of the moon, she could see a small almost heart-shaped scar just under his bottom lip. She wondered whether his wife liked to kiss him there on the scar, as she imagined herself doing.

"Do you think he suspects?" he asked.

"I don't know," she murmured.

The space between them seemed to be steadily shrinking, the heat intensifying as if an out-of-control subterranean fire were licking at their limbs. She felt acutely aware of her skin, her breasts, the gentle curve at the neckline of her gown.

Before, with Tom, it had been all about what he wanted and could teach her. His desires had ruled their lovemaking, because she'd desired nothing except that he love her. This was different. She could feel him wanting to touch her. She could feel herself longing to tell him yes, do it, touch me there . . . and there . . . and there.

"We better not take the chance," he whispered. "I should stay, in case he comes back."

His breath on her cheeks was as hot and dry as a desert wind. "Yes," she agreed, unable to tear her eyes away from his.

"Good night," he said hoarsely, licking his lips.

"Good night."

She forced herself to turn away from him and felt him doing likewise. So this is what it felt like, she thought. She ran her thumb over the gold band he'd slipped onto her ring finger. And tomorrow he would be gone from her life forever. Back to his life. To his wife. To the complications he'd said he needed to figure out. Except in her imagination, she would never know his kisses.

She put her hand to her belly, thinking of her unborn child, who would never know its father. And of all the other children, whose fathers had been stolen from them by the war. There was too much sadness and anger in the world, not enough love.

Outside, the night air thrummed with the sounds of the tiny creatures that owned the dark. She lay awake for hours, listening to the familiar songs of September, accompanied by the beating of her heart and the sound of his breath following the rhythm of hers.

He was surrounded by the thunderous din of battle—the furious rat-tat-tat of machine guns, the dull thud of hand grenades hitting their mark, the anguished cries of the wounded and dying. The night was as dark as an underground cave, the sky opaque with clouds that would explode toward dawn with a teeming rain that drenched the body and deadened the spirit.

Paul's universe had shrunk to the next few feet in front of him . . . the mud under his feet, the thick leafy branches slapping his face, the flying insects gnawing on his blood, the tips of the palm trees that towered above the smoke. By his calculations he was just within striking distance of his destination. The enemy was all around him, silent and hidden as the snakes slithering through the underbrush. He activated his flamethrower, incinerating the lush jungle greenery on either side of him. A wall of dense black smoke swirled about him, creating yet another barrier to be penetrated before he could reach his target.

He crawled forward, one painstaking inch at a time, careful to stay low, mindful that at any moment he could be felled by a bullet from an unseen enemy gun. His camouflage uniform was drenched with sweat. It felt painted onto his body. He'd volunteered for this duty, but that didn't make him any less fearful of dying. The smell of death had permeated every pore in his body, and he still hadn't figured out why any of this was happening.

Another round of flames, a scream that he could identify neither as human nor animal. He gained a few more feet. The smoke cleared and he found, too late, what he'd been searching for. The orphanage was in ruins, its outside walls and roof scorched and smoldering. The trees in front and behind were hideously blackened caricatures of themselves. The stench of burning flesh permeated the atmosphere. It seemed impossible that there could be any survivors, but he had to be sure.

Cautiously, he approached the building. A noise from within made him drop to a crouch. The door flew open. A Japanese soldier shrieked and charged through the wreckage. He leaped at Paul, his bayonet aimed to skewer Paul's heart.

Paul hit the trigger on his flamethrower. The Japanese soldier's blood-curdling battle cry became an agonizing scream of death as he disappeared in a searing flash of fire.

Through the smoke Paul saw the door swing open again. He readied himself to torch the next man out. His trigger finger was already half bent when he realized that the figure in the doorway wasn't a soldier but a ten-year-old American boy, dressed in a uniform several sizes too large for him. In his arms he was cradling a rifle that looked much too big and bulky for him to handle properly.

Confused, Paul lowered his flamethrower. The little boy lifted the rifle with the ease of a well-trained marksman, aimed, and fired. Paul shouted a warning.

The explosion jolted him instantly awake, and his terrified cry woke Victoria, as well. The nightmare stayed with him as he darted his gaze around the darkened room. The image had felt so true that his lungs still burned from the smoke of the flamethrower. He sat up in bed, trembling and gasping as he reoriented himself to reality.

Victoria switched on the light. "It's all right," she whispered, kneeling next to him.

He gulped down deep drafts of air, trying to calm his pounding heart. The horrors of the dream—the noise, the smoke, the angry little boy—gradually receded into the murk.

"It's all right," she murmured again, slipping out of bed to fetch a towel. Gently as a mother tending to a baby, she patted away the sweat on the back of his neck and stroked his head.

"It's just a dream," he muttered, as much to himself as to her. "It's nothing. It must be the change, coming home, everything so fast."

She rubbed his shoulders, uttering soft soothing noises as she probed for tension knots and kneaded them with her surprisingly strong fingers. The world slowly resumed its normal shape, though normal had never included finding himself in bed with Victoria. Her hands were lovely and cool, her skin as soft as a butterfly's wings dancing across his back.

He forgot his panic and remembered trying to fall asleep and how much he'd wanted to reach for her in the dark. Her nightgown rustled as she moved slightly away from him, reminding him of her naked-ness beneath the silk. She was the loveliest, most delicate creature on God's earth, and he would never know the taste of her lips or the smell of her against his skin. The sadness of losing what he'd never had was almost as painful as the memory of his nightmare.

The circle of light from the lamp shone like a halo around her head. Her eyes were lit with an emotion he couldn't read, or didn't dare to. Then she smiled and said, "When I was little, I would have these dreams. My mother would sing me back to sleep with this song.

"*Gracias a la vida, que me ha dado tanto*," she

began to sing in a voice so sweet it went straight to his heart. *"Que me ha dado tanto. Me dio dos luceros, que cuando los abro."*

His breath slowed, and he felt the tension seeping out of him.

Her eyes never left his as she softly translated the words into English. "Thanks to life that has given me so much. It has given me two eyes, when I open them I see you."

He felt his eyes growing heavy, his body relaxing into sleep. He fought the drowsiness, forced his eyes open again, and saw her watching him as he drifted toward stillness. She reached over and brushed back a lock of hair that had fallen across his brow.

As he slipped past consciousness, he was visited with a hazy recollection of another hand that had similarly caressed his forehead. He saw a woman's hand, a woman's voice whispering to a tiny boy frightened out of his sleep by the terrors of a night fever. . . . But it was so long ago and so dimly remembered that it might have been a figment of his imagination.

He fell into a peaceful, dreamless sleep.

He was almost immediately shocked back awake by a clanging bell that pierced the stillness with its reverberations.

"What's the matter?" he demanded of Victoria, who had already jumped out of bed and grabbed a shawl.

"Frost!" she shouted over her shoulder and ran out the door without another word.

He threw on his clothes and raced after her. The door to her bedroom was flung wide open, and he saw as he passed that Alberto and Marie Jose were already gone. Downstairs, the house was ablaze with lights hastily turned on, the servants calling to each other to hurry, get more pots and candles.

Night seemed to have turned into day. A procession of cars and trucks was lined up around the periphery, their headlights trained on the rows of night-shrouded grapes. Whole families of men, women, and children—he guessed them to be workers who lived on the property—were streaming toward the already crowded vineyard. The first arrivals, some of them still in their nightclothes, were filling the smudge pots with kerosene and unfolding translucent, wing-shaped white cotton fans.

Victoria and her mother were nowhere in sight. But Alberto stood in the thick of the action, pointing, shouting, directing the groups of workers. He whirled from one row to the next like a dervish, seemingly everywhere at once. Don Pedro hurried over and huddled with him. He shook his head and gestured toward the vines, then turned and looked out at the fields.

The workers whose smudge pots were already filled stood at the edge of the vineyards, as if awaiting a signal. Suddenly, a man appeared running from the middle of the rows, holding a bunch of grapes high above his head like a trophy.

Paul moved in closer and saw the man hand the grapes to Alberto, who scrutinized them with the care of a scientist. He touched first one, then another, then yet a third. By the light of the cars, Paul could see that crystals of frost had formed on the outside of the bunch. But when Alberto plucked a grape from the middle, the purple skin was devoid of even a single drop of moisture.

"It hasn't reached the inside!" Alberto shouted. "We can still save them! We have a chance! Now!"

The general had summoned the infantry into battle. The workers sprang into action, simultaneously lighting their smudge pots. With the precision of a well-trained team, they marched single file between the rows, a sinuous human glowworm breathing clouds of smoke to stave off the potentially murderous frost.

The urgency of the situation was obvious even to an outsider like Paul. The entire crop might be lost if they couldn't raise the temperature in the vineyard above freezing. With no grapes to be harvested, no wine would be produced this year. The Aragons— and the many families employed by them—stood to lose the entire basis of their annual income.

Paul rushed over to Alberto. "How can I help?" he asked.

Alberto glared at him as if he were the one to blame for the early frost. He turned away to speak to one of his workers, then seemed to have a change of heart. He scooped up a pair of the large winglike fans and pushed it at Paul.

"You know how to fly?"

Paul clumsily unfolded the two pieces of triangularly cut fabric, which were shaped and held together by wire spokes like those of an umbrella. "If you'll show me," he said.

"We're going to lose everything and you want me to take time to show you?"

Alberto slapped his thigh in disgust. Clearly, his new son-in-law was proving every bit the no-account failure he'd suspected him of being. That Paul had never stepped foot in a vineyard before, much less sprouted wings and learned to fly was of no interest to him. A chocolate salesman who'd been raised in an orphanage had no place in his vineyard, especially when the fate of the harvest was at stake. Plunging into the billows of smoke that rose from the smudge pots, he stomped off to inspect the progress of his workers.

"Slowly! Even! Even!" he yelled.

Though it was hard to say for sure, Paul chose to believe that the precious few words of instruction were meant for him, not the workers. He held the wings aloft and tried to figure out how they were meant to be used. Certainly, Alberto couldn't have been serious about Paul flying. So what exactly was the purpose of the wings, and how was he supposed to work them?

"Like a butterfly," said Victoria, coming up behind him.

She was wearing a pair of the wings herself. Her arms were hooked through a small space between the gauzy fabric and the spokes that supported and gave shape to the wings. She flapped the wings in a careful rhythm, fanning the air as she raised and lowered her arms. Watching her, he understood. The wings were needed to fan the smoke from the smudge pots.

Despite the chill in the air, she was dressed only in her nightgown. The sight of her breasts rising and falling beneath the thin silky gown as she worked the fans took his breath away. With her white wings and long neck, she looked as graceful as a swan. It would have surprised him not at all if she'd suddenly taken flight.

He inserted his arms into his pair and tried to imitate her. But she'd made the motion look far easier than it was. He couldn't fall into a rhythm; his movements were jerky and awkward. If she was a swan, he was a lumbering, earthbound bear. He couldn't reproduce the synchronized dip of her arms, the even flow of air she'd so effortlessly accomplished.

He went and stood behind her, and she showed him again, this time more slowly, how to dip the wings, then slightly rotate his arms backward. When she tilted her head up to smile her encouragement, he almost couldn't keep from kissing her. Her bare shoulders shimmered like a mirage. They begged to be caressed, if only he dared.

She nodded her approval. Yes, he had it now, more or less. She could spare no more time to teach him. "Get the heat down on the grapes," she said before she went to join the other workers.

Then, "Butterfly," she called to him, naming

herself, a radiant silken-skinned vision. The beams from the cars shone through the fabric of her gown, highlighting her supple body. Paralyzed with desire, he stared after her as she moved through the vineyard with the sensual liquidity of a dancer, beating the smoke and heat down into the vines.

Alberto caught him in the act. "If you're going to help, help!" he snarled from across a row of vines.

He quickly raised his arms and entered the vineyard. Up and down, forward and dip, he reminded himself—like a butterfly. But his clumsy attempt to fan the wings only succeeded in driving the smoke up into his face. He felt as if he were choking on the pungent vapors and began coughing so violently that he totally lost his concentration.

Alberto scowled with unconcealed contempt and stalked off to check on another section of the vineyard.

"Follow me," Victoria called to him from the next row. "Up . . . down. Up . . . down." She flapped her wings in long sweeping strokes, her whole body undulating to the languid rhythm she'd set for herself.

Determined now, he began again, silently counting out a beat he could follow as he pushed down and dipped back. It was like waltzing. All he had to do was keep track of the tempo and think of the wings as a partner who needed to be led across the floor of the dance hall.

He imagined himself dancing with Victoria, one arm around her back, one hand clasping hers. In the background the band played sweet, romantic tunes, and the lights were turned down low, so that it seemed as if they were the only two people in the room. She was smiling at him, and then she moved closer and rested her head on his shoulder, and he could feel her breasts pressing against his chest. "Let's do this forever," she whispered, and his heart swelled with joy. Yes, he nodded, knowing he could happily spend forever with Victoria.

Stirred by his fantasy, he discovered that he was able to maintain a more even, deliberate stroke. His movements were slowly becoming more coordinated as his body adapted to the rhythm he'd set for himself. With each beat of his wings, he drove the smoke down toward the grapes, forcing more of the heat to be trapped there among the vines.

"Yes, that's it!" Victoria cheered him on. "Come on! With me!" she sang out as he caught up with her.

She turned toward him, her gossamer-thin nightgown clinging to her body. He followed her lead, marveling at the ease with which she manipulated the fans. Setting his pace to hers, he soon found that he could move more quickly and with less effort. Gradually, they began to beat their wings in unison, their bodies rising and falling in perfect syncopation, like lovers anticipating each other's movements. Their movements flowed one with the other, playing out the dance of passion they couldn't admit to in words. The smoke swirled around them, and their frosted breath mingled in the chill night air as beat by beat, they lost themselves in the dance.

The others came and went, moving along the rows, but Paul and Victoria had eyes only for each other. Absorbed as they were, they failed to see that Alberto was watching them through the haze of smoke that hovered like a cloud above the vast field. Once the immediate crisis had passed, he had stopped to survey his domain, to check whether more smudge pots were needed, where the fans could be put to best use.

Like radar scanning the skies for signs of trouble, he'd picked up a disturbing blip on the screen, and his gaze had settled there to assess the situation. He tugged at his mustache, his dark brows beetling as he scowled his displeasure. From his expression at that moment, it would have been difficult to guess which concerned him more—the early frost that threatened his crop, or his daughter's choice of husband.

The workers didn't leave the vineyard until just before the first light of day. The Aragons were the last to go, and even then, Alberto insisted on staying behind to stand guard. Against what, he couldn't say, when Marie Jose asked him why he couldn't come back to bed for a couple of hours. It had always been so, as far back as Victoria remembered. Her father loved the grapes with the same fierce intensity that he loved his children. They needed to be safeguarded at all costs, worried over, occasionally pampered, preserved from harm.

His family left him there and wearily straggled back to the house. No one spoke, least of all Paul and Victoria, not even when they were alone again in the privacy of her parents' bedroom. They were exhausted and exhilarated, thrilled and saddened beyond words. They couldn't speak their feelings, but the truth showed on their faces as clearly as the black streaks from the smoke.

The merest sliver of sun had appeared behind the eastern mountains, and the sky was an opalescent pearl-gray. Paul was wiping away the last of the smudges when he looked out the window and saw Alberto, still patroling the rows with his lantern, poking between the vines, ever vigilant.

For once, he looked at peace. Paul could see his lips moving, as if he were telling the grapes, "You're safe now."

He leaned farther out the window and heard Alberto singing to the vines. The words of the song drifted through the hush of dawn, the same song Victoria had sung to comfort him.

"Gracias a la vida, que me ha dado tanto. . . ."

And then he saw Alberto raise his head and catch sight of him there in the window. Alberto's expression darkened, and the song died in his throat.

CHAPTER

· 7 ·

Victoria sat on the bed, watching Paul button up his shirt and put on his jacket. The intimacy of the moment didn't escape her, and it felt all the more precious because this would be their first—and only—such morning together. She'd thought her heart had been broken by Tom's desertion, but whatever she'd felt then couldn't compare to the sense of utter desolation washing over her now.

The hours just past had been time out of time, moments of magic that glistened and shimmered like drops of dew in the early morning sunlight. She knew with unwavering certainty that she'd found her *caballero*. With equal certainty she knew that he could never be hers except in her mind's eye.

If there was anything she could have done or said to stop him, she would have done or said it. She would have begged and pleaded and cajoled. But his every gesture and expression told her he didn't want to leave any more than she wanted him to. That if there were any way to do this differently, he would.

"I'll leave the letter saying I've abandoned you in the mailbox," he said, holding up the paper that would condemn him forever in the eyes of her family.

She twirled a thread that was coming loose from the pillow case. "The bus doesn't leave until eleven A.M."

But he had his plan all figured out, structured to make things easier for both of them. "Then it's daylight. Everyone will be up. It's better this way. Fewer questions."

"Yes." She nodded sadly. He was right. And yet . . .

"Victoria." He sighed as he picked up his hat. "I have to go."

She lay the flat of her hand against her stomach. There was so much she yearned to say and couldn't. "I know. I just wish . . ."

They looked at each other, and their eyes said it all for them—the longing, the passion, the love, the knowing that they were two halves of a whole.

"I wish you the best of luck," she said finally.

She fought her tears as he picked up his duffel bag and sample case. There had to be something she could say . . . some way to change the ending of this story about two people who so obviously belonged together.

Maybe his wife had forgotten to mention she was already married, and now her first husband wanted her back. Maybe she had fallen madly in love with another man and was waiting for him to call so she could tell him the news. Maybe she had suddenly gotten very religious and gone off to join a nunnery. Or maybe grapes had started crushing themselves into wine and pigs could talk.

He swallowed hard, gulping back his sadness. "Best of luck to you, too," he said, and then he was gone.

The mist that came at dawn from the other side of the mountains had settled over the vineyard, shrouding the rows of grapes like a veil of gauze. In an hour or so, as soon as the sun rose, it would be gone, dissipated by the heat of the day. Already, the higher ground of the surrounding hills was clearly visible in the distance, each tree and bush distinctly outlined in the thin early morning light.

His letter in hand, Paul stood on the porch of the hacienda to take a last look at the mountains. When he heard the door open, he turned around, hoping it would be Victoria, come to kiss him good-bye. Instead, he found himself face-to-face with Don Pedro, dressed in a battered tan fedora and a plaid robe he'd thrown over his nightclothes.

"It is the call of the grapes that robs our sleep," he said, rubbing the stubble on his chin. "When they are ripe, they call to a man." He stretched his arms above his head and inhaled deeply. "Walk with me," he said, stepping off the porch.

It was an order, not an invitation. Paul felt he had no choice but to obey Victoria's grandfather.

"Bring the chocolates," Don Pedro added as he sauntered into the mist.

Paul thought briefly about his eleven o'clock bus and his plan to get away from *Las Nubes* before the rest of the house woke up. Then he picked up his chocolate sampler and followed Don Pedro down the path to the vineyard. The mist lay low to the ground, reaching only as far as his knees, giving the illusion that they were walking through a bank of vaporous clouds.

He strolled silently alongside Don Pedro. The smell of kerosene still hung in the air, and here and there he saw a smudge pot that hadn't been collected. Otherwise, there was no evidence of the well-organized campaign that had been conducted only a few hours earlier. Under other circumstances he might have enjoyed sharing these few minutes of solitude with Don Pedro, who, more than anyone else, had befriended him. But the letter in his pocket was like a thorn whose sharp nettles couldn't be ignored, no matter how hard he tried not to think about it.

"The doctors say, 'No chocolate, Don Pedro. No salt, Don Pedro. No cigars. Not too much brandy.' What the hell does a doctor know about the needs of a man's soul?" Don Pedro peered at Paul, then succinctly answered his own question. *"Nada!"*

He pointed to Paul's sampler. "May I?"

Mr. Sweeney's training manual explicitly forbade giving out samples to anyone who wasn't a bona fide potential account, and this would make two that Don Pedro had taken. But he looked so eager, so much like a little boy staring into the candy store window, that Paul decided to report the missing chocolates as an investment in possible word-of-mouth advertising.

He held the case open. Just as he'd done the night before, Don Pedro took his time making his choice. His mind finally made up, he selected a piece that was wrapped with a gold band identical to the one Paul had given Victoria to use as her wedding ring. He slipped off the band and examined it closely.

"It looks just like my granddaughter's," he said.

Paul snatched the band out of his hand and pretended to study it. "I never noticed that," he said.

Don Pedro stared at him for what seemed like a very long minute. Then he popped the chocolate, a caramel mint, into his mouth and rolled it around on his tongue, savoring every morsel of it. *"Excelente!"* he pronounced it.

Without bothering to ask, he picked out another piece, this one a marshmallow fudge, and walked on toward the vineyard.

The rows of vines began only a few yards away from the hacienda, at a point at which the land declined slightly. Because the vineyard fell in a valley within a valley, the mist got trapped longer. The cloud was so thick there that Paul could hardly make out the vines on either side of the muddy pathway.

"In 1580, the first Aragon, also a Pedro, came from Spain to Mexico," said Don Pedro. "With a dream in his head, the clothes on his back, and a

root from the family's vineyard inside his pocket."
He nodded at the sampler. "May I?"

Don Pedro was the perfect example of a satisfied
customer. It was nice to find a man who appreciated
fine chocolate and ate it with such gusto. Paul
wished he could introduce him to Mr. Sweeney,
whom he had begun to feel had lost touch with his
clientele. "Be my guest," he said.

This time Don Pedro went straight for the walnut cream, one of Paul's favorites. "Wonderful," he
declared. He shook his head, seeming to marvel at
the superiority of Paul's wares.

"For centuries," he said dreamily, reciting his
family history as if it had been told and retold many
times over the years, "the vineyard produced wine of
such character that it graced the best tables in all
Mexico. And then the revolution . . ."

He sighed, then fell silent. Paul wanted to hear
more but said nothing, waiting for him to continue
when he was ready. He sensed that Don Pedro was
lost in the past, reliving some terrible hurt that
hadn't ever healed, not even after all these years.

He felt a stab of sympathy for the old man; he
knew about hurt and sadness that could never en-
tirely be forgotten and never really went away. It
seemed to come from losing something that once had
been very precious. So that no matter what you
did—no matter where you looked—you could never
replace whatever it was that you'd lost. Not even
when once in a very great while you thought you'd

happened upon someone who would replace that nameless thing missing from your life.

"We escaped with our lives," Don Pedro continued, helping himself without asking to another chocolate. "One suitcase of clothes, and in my pocket, a root from the vineyard."

Paul tried to imagine a much younger Don Pedro, not much older than he was now, fleeing with Guadalupe across the Mexican border. He glanced around, trying to get his bearings, wondering how far he was from the hacienda and the road that led to the other side of the hills. Here the clouds of mist were so dense that he could see only vague shadows and shapes.

A fragment from his nightmare came into his mind: an image of himself crawling through a cloud of smoke, searching out the enemy. Nothing was clear. He was all alone and walking blind.

"I will show you something," Don Pedro said suddenly, leading him farther into the mists.

They walked for some distance, climbing a slight incline. Paul could see a brilliant orange sun cresting the hills behind him, and below stood the vineyard, still hidden beneath clouds. On the higher ground, where the mist had already begun to dissolve, the lush vines strained under the weight of the grapes, ripe for the harvest.

Don Pedro pointed to a single vine, ancient and gnarled, that was set apart from the others. Behind it was what appeared to be a modest shrine, a weathered headstone with two short sentences inscribed in Spanish. His hands clasped behind his back, Don Pedro gazed at the site and at the hills that sloped across the landscape beyond.

"This is the root I brought with me," he said. "Descended from the root the first Pedro brought with him. It is not just the root of *Las Nubes*. It is the root of our lives . . . of Victoria's life." He turned and looked into Paul's face. "And now that you are part of this—part of us—it is the root of your life. You are an orphan no longer."

His words struck Paul at his core. Though it hadn't always been so, he knew himself only as an orphan. He'd been left at the orphanage as an infant, with no note of explanation or keepsake to connect him with his mother or father. He couldn't even guess at the identity of his parents, though like almost every other child in the institution he'd created an elaborate family tree—crowded with aunts, uncles, cousins, grandparents—all of whom he was certain would happily take him in, if only they knew where he was.

Don Pedro had offered him the family he'd always wanted—and so much more. A history, a home, a piece of land whose beauty was unsurpassed, especially at this moment, with the rising sun casting its golden glow across the endless rows of vines.

The mist had fallen away, revealing the valley in its full glory, and the hacienda, set down in the middle of it all, like a gem at the center of a priceless piece of jewelry. He'd spent not even a day there, but already he'd learned so much more about families than he'd ever known. Families weren't all either good or evil, black and white, as he'd believed them to be. They were subject to turbulent tides of emotions, to strong currents pulling this way and that.

"So. You will stay with your family for the harvest of the fruit?" asked Don Pedro. "It is a special time. A time of magic."

He realized then that Don Pedro had noticed his duffel bag on the porch and correctly assumed that he was leaving. He wondered what else the old man had surmised about his unannounced arrival at *Las Nubes*. If only he could stay. If only the magic of the harvest were powerful enough to wipe out the past, erase his marriage to Betty, so that the Aragons truly could be his family.

"I really can't," he said mournfully. "I have commitments."

Don Pedro raised his face to the sun, allowing its warmth to play over his craggy features. "And what about the commitment to your family? What can be more important than that?"

Nothing could have made him happier than to say yes, of course, he would stay. But Betty was his family now, and his commitment had to be to her. He shook his head. "I would like to, really. But I can't."

Don Pedro shrugged his shoulders, resigned. "He said you wouldn't stay."

"Who did?"

"Alberto. 'The first chance the gringo gets he will leave her.' His exact words." He bent down to pluck some weeds that had grown up around the headstone.

Paul guiltily fingered the letter in his pocket. "I'm not leaving her."

"I understand." Don Pedro brushed the dirt off his hands.

Paul wondered how much he truly did understand. He sensed that unlike Alberto, who made no secret of his emotions, Don Pedro kept hidden much of what he was thinking or feeling.

"It's just my poor granddaughter—he will whip her with it. She'll be the one to pay for your commitments. A pity. Such a sweet girl." He sighed and turned to go back down to the hacienda, where some of the workers had already begun to gather.

Paul quickly caught up with him. "But it would just be the difference of a day," he said, torn between desire and obligation.

"The most important day of our year. The day that makes or breaks our fortunes. That's what he will throw up to her. For the rest of her life. Knowing my son . . ."

He couldn't live with knowing that he'd made the situation worse, not better, for Victoria. George Sweeney and the candy stores in Sacramento had waited four years for him; they could wait another day if it would truly make such a difference for Victoria's future happiness. In the scheme of things, how could it possibly matter?

"Don Pedro," he said. "You're right. It's only one day. I'll stay."

Don Pedro didn't seem at all surprised by Paul's decision. He grinned and pointed to the sampler case. "It's a good thing." He chuckled. "You have no more chocolates to sell anyway."

Paul flipped open the top of his case. Don Pedro had eaten every piece of chocolate except for the Wedding Bon Bon Deluxe, which he now reached over to rescue from its lonely splendor in the middle of the box. He popped it into his mouth and flashed Paul a wide, contented smile.

A bell clanged across the valley. The sun was up. It was time to get to work. There were grapes to be harvested.

The area at the edge of the vineyard was crowded with people and equipment. Horse-drawn flatbed wagons stood at the ready. Empty grape boxes were stacked at the beginning of each row of vines. Smaller baskets hung from the arms of the pickers, some of whom lived year-round in the valley, and others who traveled the state following the crop harvests. Almost everyone seemed to know one another, and to share Don Pedro's excitement about the day.

Children darted in and out among the wagons. Their parents greeted old friends they hadn't seen in months. Soon the back-breaking hours of labor would begin and there'd be no time or energy for chatting. But many of the pickers had worked for Don Pedro since he'd harvested his very first crop of grapes, and he was considered one of the most honorable of the grape growers in the valley. They were pleased to return to the Aragon vineyard, where the wages were fair, the food plentiful, and no one worked harder or longer than Don Pedro and the rest of his family.

Alberto had already taken himself off to the vineyard, and Victoria was just coming out of the house when Don Pedro and Paul returned from their early morning stroll. She was carrying a stack of the picking baskets, which she almost dropped in surprise when she saw Paul coming up to the porch to meet her.

"I thought you were leaving," she whispered.

Paul decided not to mention his conversation with Don Pedro. Despite his earlier hesitation, he was glad to be here now and knew he'd made the correct choice. Don Pedro had counseled him wisely. He'd offered his help to Victoria, and he couldn't run out on her at the moment she most needed him.

"I thought it would be better for you if I stuck around at least until the harvest," he said quietly.

He was rewarded for his act of kindness with a look of profound love and appreciation. He smiled back at her, wishing there were some way he could permanently shield her from Alberto's criticism and anger.

"Don't you have chocolates to sell?" said Alberto, coming up to them with a bunch of grapes in his hand. His eyes were hard and wary. Nothing Paul did could please him. Whether he stayed or left, he was still the orphan from Moline with no prospects, who had no business insinuating himself into Victoria's affections.

Aware of Alberto's opinions, Paul cast about for the right answer. The only explanation that made any sense was the one Don Pedro had just given him. "Family comes first," he said.

Victoria smiled and glanced sideways at her father to gauge his response. Alberto was not easily mollified, however. From his expression, it was clear to Paul that he had more to say on the subject of Paul's presence.

He was distracted from further expressing himself by the sight of a car raising a flurry of dust as it jolted down the road and stopped in front of the house. With a blare of the horn the last missing member of the Aragon family announced his arrival.

"Pedro!" shouted Victoria, running to hug her younger brother.

Pedro Alberto Aragon-Limantour jumped out of his shiny red convertible and threw his arms around Victoria.

"Hiya, sis!" he whooped as the others crowded around to greet him and welcome him home.

Pedro's face was a softer, younger version of his father's. But he was dressed like a college boy, and he looked the part of the all-American campus hero in his round glasses, stylishly slicked-back hair, and saddle shoes.

"*Hola*, Pedro!" Don Pedro embraced his grandson and namesake.

"Hi, Grandpa! Hi, Grandma!" He kissed Guadalupe. "My favorite chillies ready?"

"*Claro que sí, Pedrito!*" She hugged him warmly. Of course, she'd made chillies for him.

A kiss for Marie Jose, and a clap on the back for Alberto, then he said breezily, "Hi, Mom. Hi, Pop. Sorry I'm late!"

Finally, he noticed the stranger standing next to his sister.

"Pedro," said Victoria, anticipating his questions. "This is my husband, Paul Sutton. Paul, my brother."

"You got hitched?"

She nodded and managed a weak smile. Paul steeled himself for Pedro's reaction, but Victoria's brother surprised him.

"Hey, that's great!" he declared. "Victoria Sutton! I like that!" He thrust out his hand. "Welcome to the family. I'm Pete."

"Pete?" Alberto snorted. "Who is Pete?" he demanded.

"Aw, Pa, c'mon . . ." Pedro said, embarrassed.

Alberto glared at his son. "I don't know any Pete. I know I pay a fortune in tuition to Stanford University for a Pedro Alberto Aragon-Limantour. Maybe I am paying for the wrong person, and I should stop the check."

Pedro scowled but said nothing. Caught in the crossfire between father and son, Paul waited for someone to break the tense silence that had fallen over the family. He was shocked by Alberto's outburst. What a terrible homecoming he had given his son, who had driven all his way, only to be publicly chastised for something as insignificant as an Americanized nickname. It was no wonder Victoria had been so fearful of telling her father that she was pregnant and unmarried.

But Alberto wasn't his father, and he had no reason to be afraid of him. A rhyme he remembered from childhood ran through his head: *Sticks and stones can break my bones, but words can never hurt me.* If the Japanese hadn't managed to fell him with their bullets, Alberto Aragon certainly couldn't kill him with his barbs, well-aimed though they were.

"Glad to meet you, Pedro," he said, shaking his hand.

Everyone except Alberto seemed to breathe a collective sigh of relief. Marie Jose smiled and lovingly patted Pedro's cheek. Don Pedro winked at Paul behind Alberto's back as he reached into the car to grab his grandson's bags.

Alberto waved his hands in disgust. First his daughter, now his son had disappointed him. They were a generation that held nothing sacred. "Can we begin now?" he bellowed. "Or are we going to wait for the grapes to turn to raisins? Come on!"

The crowd needed no further urging. Men, women, and children rushed toward the vineyard, grabbing equipment as they entered the rows. The youngsters, who were responsible for collecting the bunches of grapes that fell to the ground, carried smaller versions of their parents' baskets. Alberto's three chief assistants moved among the workers, making certain that everyone knew the area to which he or she had been assigned.

"Victoria!" Alberto beckoned to his daughter. "Make sure he knows what he is doing. We don't want him cutting off his fingers and getting blood on the grapes. It'll ruin the taste of the wine."

Pleased with himself for having gotten the last laugh, he handed her a pair of cutting shears and went to join Don Pedro.

Even Alberto's nastiness couldn't ruin the joy of the day for Victoria. Her brother—her best friend and ally—was home. The harvest celebration awaited them. Best of all, Paul was still there with her, if only for another day.

"Aren't you glad you stayed?" she said, laughing and shaking her head as she watched her father disappear into the field. Then she flashed Paul a mischievous smile and, deliberately exaggerating the sway of her hips, she followed Alberto into the vineyard.

CHAPTER

· 8 ·

Just as the quality and flavor of the wines they produced differed from one Napa Valley winery to the next, so did the mood and tempo of their harvests. At *Las Nubes*, where Don Pedro still reigned as the master wine maker, there was a sense of camaraderie among the pickers. They felt a loyalty toward Don Pedro, who knew each one of them by name. He flirted with the women and filled his pockets with candy for the children. And he sent every family home at the end of the harvest with a bottle of the same wine that his family drank at their table.

Thanks to Don Pedro's influence, and in spite of Alberto's dour character, the mood in the Aragon vineyard was usually festive and convivial. There was much calling back and forth between the rows, good-natured teasing, and offers of bets to be taken as to who could fill the most baskets. And the

Aragons worked right alongside everyone else until the very last grape was picked and crushed.

The process of picking the grapes was like a well-choreographed dance: They were removed bunch by bunch from the vines and collected either in various-sized baskets or boxes. The heavy containers then had to be carried to the end of each row so that they could be loaded onto the horse-drawn carts. The grapes were then delivered to the huge crushing vats, where Don Pedro himself supervised the transfer of the grapes from the carts into the vats. This step of the process took more than sheer muscle. A sharp eye was required, to ensure that only the sweetest, juiciest grapes were unloaded. The reputation of the winery could be tarnished for years to come by even one batch of sour, contaminating grapes.

It didn't take long for the familiar rhythms to be reestablished, and the workers were soon busy at their various jobs. Paul felt like the odd man out, the only one in the crowd who couldn't seem to cut the grapes cleanly, without spraying juice all over himself and everyone else. The temperature had begun to soar with the rising sun. His shirt stuck to his back, sweat was soaking his neck, and his hands were wet and slippery. The shears were hard to handle, and the vines were surprisingly thick, so that it took a good deal more effort than he would have expected to sever the bunches.

And now that you are a part of us. . . . Don Pedro's words echoed in his mind. But he wasn't, and he never would be a part of what was happening all around him. Even the smallest child seemed to be more adept than he at harvesting the grapes. He was the outsider, the city slicker who'd shed his tie and jacket but still looked out of place in his salesman's suit. A burst of laughter interrupted his thoughts; he looked around and saw young Pedro flirting with one of the pickers. Pedro, who was also Pete, depending on the situation. So perhaps a person could find a way to fit in and be comfortable with himself even in unfamiliar settings.

There was no reason he couldn't pick grapes as fast as anyone else in the vineyard, he decided. He wiped his hands dry on his pants and renewed his attack. But he was distracted again, this time by what felt like a grape bouncing off his forehead. He glanced up and saw Victoria, pretty as a bouquet of daisies in her flowered sundress and simple straw hat, smiling at him from the next row. She looked as if she was actually enjoying herself, which made him feel more cheerful.

He winked and held up the bunch he'd just cut, showing it off to her like a trophy. But he paid for his pride when the next bunch he cut slipped out of his hands and tumbled to the ground just as Alberto was coming around the corner. Paul grabbed for the grapes, but Alberto got there first. He glared at Paul dismissively, as if accusing him of single-handedly undermining the harvest, brushed the dirt off the fruit, and threw the bunch into Paul's box.

Then he stepped past him to the next row and began to fill up his own empty box, cutting the vines with a quick, precise flick of his wrist. Alberto was like a master craftsman, working at maximum efficiency with a minimum of wasted time and motion. There was a kind of beauty to the way he performed the difficult but mundane task. He seemed almost to caress the grapes with one hand as he clipped the vine with the other. Suddenly, Paul recalled how Alberto had walked the vineyard before dawn, whispering softly and singing to the fruit of his labor. All this was his, he seemed to be saying to Paul now. He could have none of it, neither Victoria nor the joy of participating in the harvest.

But I can and will, Paul decided. He willed himself to concentrate, modeling his motions after Alberto's, trying to match him movement for movement. He made it into a game in his head; he gave himself a point if he succeeded in cutting one bunch for every two that Alberto picked. His pace picked up as he relaxed into the rhythm, and his box began to fill up with grapes.

Alberto had already filled one box to the brim and was working on his second. He stopped to drink some water, noticed Paul working feverishly, and smiled smugly. Undeterred, Paul kept on going, determined to catch up, even overtake him, if possible.

The sun was almost directly overhead. Soon the lunch bell would ring, and the workers would take an hour to eat and rest in the shade. With so much ground still to be covered, there was less talk now, more calls for boxes, empty baskets, water. Paul was picking like an expert now, harvesting at a good steady clip. He was oblivious to the heat, his thirst, the other workers, to everything except his goal of besting Alberto.

From the next row over, Alberto saw what Paul was up to. He redoubled his efforts, rushing to finish his vine so he could move ahead to the next one. He was done a few seconds ahead of Paul, but Paul was gaining on him, now only three vines behind, cutting the bunches with a precision that rivaled Alberto's.

The other workers nudged one another and whispered down the rows about the unspoken contest being fought between Alberto and the gringo. Victoria dropped her basket and stood with Marie Jose and Guadalupe; the three women watched in amazement as Paul closed in on Alberto. Don Pedro, too, took notice of the competition and called a temporary halt at the vats, as the two men, master and novice, raced to the finish line.

Two vines behind, another box filled. Paul was catching up. Undaunted, Alberto moved on to the last vine in the row. He was drenched in sweat and breathing hard, like a long-distance runner coming in to his final mile. Now Paul was only one vine behind, cutting bunches as if he'd been harvesting all his life. Alberto's pride was at stake. He would rather have died right there in the vineyard than let Paul finish first.

His hands moved from the vine to the basket without a single wasted motion, as efficiently as a well-oiled machine. Slice and toss. Slice and toss. His box was full, but he had no time to spare waiting for an empty one. The bunches of grapes were spilling over the sides of the box, glistening with the sweat from his fingers.

Only half a vine ahead of Paul, and his hands were cramping with fatigue. The shears almost slipped from his grasp. He grunted, grabbed them more tightly, and sliced off the very last bunch on the vine. When he tossed it onto the already overflowing pile, it teetered on the edge, then toppled over into the dirt.

"Listo!" he cried. He was finished, ready, done!

A triumphant shout rose through the vineyard. Alberto held his arms aloft like a prizefighter, grinning from ear to ear with satisfaction. There were few things he enjoyed more in life than a good fight, and this victory was especially sweet for having been achieved at his son-in-law's expense. Rivers of sweat ran across his face and down his body. He was delighted with himself, exhausted, and very thirsty. When one of the foremen tossed him a wineskin, he tipped it to his mouth and slaked his thirst with several very long and noisy gulps.

Paul waited, catching his breath, until Alberto was finished drinking. In spite of losing, he'd enjoyed the game. But it wasn't over yet. He reached down in front of Alberto and grabbed the bunch of grapes that had fallen out of the box onto the ground. Then he dusted them off, just as Alberto had done earlier with the bunch he'd picked, and carefully positioned them on top of the pile.

Alberto seemed to appreciate the joke. He favored

him with a slight smile, then sealed his grudging approval by offering him a drink from the wineskin. Paul caught Victoria's eye as he lifted the skin to his lips. She was beaming with pleasure, and he was smiling as well, even though he managed to spill much more of the wine down the front of his shirt than he squirted down his throat. For once, coming in second felt like a first-place victory.

Paul's shirt and pants were so stained with red wine and perspiration that as soon as the bell rang to signal the end of the day's work, Guadalupe hustled him off to the house to find him a clean set of clothes. Laughing at his predicament, she pulled out of her husband's dresser a faded cotton plaid shirt and a pair of worn trousers. Then she pushed Paul into the bathroom, handed him a towel, and told him to leave his dirty things in the basket on the floor so that someone would wash them.

By the time he came back outside, he saw in the fading light that the area around the crushing vats was abuzz with activity. Hoping to find Victoria there, he strolled toward the vineyard. He was way-laid by Don Pedro, who smiled at the sight of him, dressed in his old familiar clothes.

"How do they feel?" he asked.

Paul laughed as he rolled up his shirtsleeves. "They're a little big."

Don Pedro stepped back to inspect him, then fiddled with his suspenders, adjusted the collar, buttoned a button. "Clothes are like family," he said. "You have to live in them for a while before you get a perfect fit. You're doing great."

Paul glanced over at Alberto, who stood where Don Pedro had held court earlier in the day, supervising the unloading of the grapes into the vats. "I don't know if everyone would share your opinion," he said ruefully.

"It is not easy being in charge," Don Pedro said. He watched his son urge the workers to hurry up, move faster. "It was not easy for me. It is not easy for him. But every man finds his own way. I have faith in my son."

He sighed as he turned back to Paul and held his gaze, as if he were studying his soul. "I have faith in you," he said. He grinned and pointed to Paul's crotch. "Your fly."

Paul bent his head to fasten his zipper. When he looked up again, Don Pedro had already strolled back to the vats to resume his duties. Paul watched him conferring with Alberto, who shook his head, then walked away to speak to one of the foremen.

"So what do you think?" asked young Pedro, coming over to join him. He was carrying two glasses of wine, one of which he offered to Paul.

"I like it . . . everyone working together. It reminds me of the army."

"Yeah. I just wish I could get the general over there to listen instead of giving orders all the time." Pedro nodded at his father, who was still busy giving orders.

"There's going to be a revolution in this business, and it's going to happen without us. We should be at the forefront. If he'd just give in and modernize . . . I mean, look at this." He gestured to the crushing vats, the horse-drawn carts, the workers with their straw baskets. "We're stuck in the Middle Ages."

Paul sipped the wine. It felt dry on his tongue and tasted of spices. "Have you tried talking to him?"

"Have you?" Pedro raised an eyebrow, finished his wine, and walked away.

Paul stayed to finish his wine and to watch the knots of people still gathered at the edge of the vineyard and around the hacienda. In the lavender light of dusk, with the fruity aroma of the grapes hanging in the air, it all seemed so tranquil and perfect. A paradise, he'd thought yesterday, catching his first glimpse of the valley from the top of the hill. Yet each generation chafed at the restrictions imposed by the one previous, and change was in the air. He didn't have to take Pedro's word for it. He knew that himself from having been to war.

He was pulled back from his musings about what the future might bring to *Las Nubes* by a clamor of loud voices and the utterly improbable sight of Guadalupe, flying through the air above the crowd, clutching a conch shell in her hand. The workers clapped and called out to her as they surged forward toward the vats. He hurried after them, elbowing his way through. Close up, he saw that Guadalupe had actually been carried across the field on the shoulders of four men, who were now helping her climb down into the center of the largest of the vats.

A hush fell over the vineyard even before she raised the conch shell to her mouth and blew into its curved opening. The sound she created had a hollow, haunting quality that seemed to come from another world. He searched the crowd until he found Victoria, but before he could make his way over to ask her what was happening, Guadalupe turned to face the south and blew into the shell again.

"My wife's people, the Aztec," said Don Pedro, coming over to join him. "It is their belief . . ."

Guadalupe turned to the east and let go another blast that echoed in Paul's heart.

". . . we must ask permission of the four winds to harvest what the earth gives," Don Pedro murmured. He stared at his wife as she repeated the ceremony, turning next to the north, then finally to the west, looking into the sunset.

"She is still so beautiful," he said, his eyes shining with love.

The last note from the shell lingered in the air until it was carried away by the wind. A long silence followed, and then Don Pedro's booming voice shattered the stillness. "*Las mujeres!*" he proclaimed.

The women cheered in response to his summons. One after another, they found their husbands, grabbed them by their hands, and rushed toward the vat where Guadalupe stood, her arms outstretched like a goddess welcoming her subjects. Marie Jose was among the first to take her place there, with Alberto standing right behind her.

"Victoria!" she called to her daughter, who hung back as the other women hurried past her. "Come! You're a wife now!"

All afternoon Victoria had been thinking about this very moment. It should have been one of the highlights of her young life—her first harvest as a married woman, participating in a ritual as ancient as the one her grandmother had just celebrated. Except that . . . she wasn't married. She had no right to dance with the other women. But there was no excuse she could offer not to dance. And just this one time, she wished it could be so. She wished she could be Paul's wife. For just this one magical night.

The force of her wish carried her over to Paul. It gave her the courage to take his hand and lead him to the vat.

"What about Pedro?" he said, still not understanding.

"He's not married," she muttered.

"Neither are we," he whispered.

A smile hid the pain his words caused her. She took her place around the vat with the rest of the women, directing Paul to stand a few inches behind her alongside the other men.

At a nod from Guadalupe, the women kicked off their shoes and hiked their skirts up to the top of their legs. Victoria grabbed Paul's hands and placed them on either side of her waist, as the other couples had done. Past caring about what was right or wrong, she boldly met his gaze and wordlessly dared him to take a good long look at her, to enjoy the sight of her bare legs and thighs.

Their eyes locked. Suddenly, nothing else existed in their universe. It was just the two of them, all alone. Nothing could come between them. No one could spoil their happiness. No one could thwart the consummation of their love.

"Uno! Dos! Tres!" shouted Don Pedro.

The spell was broken.

The world crowded in on them again. A beat behind the others, Paul lifted her up by the waist and swung her over the rim of the vat onto the mass of soft, ripe grapes. She squealed as her bare feet hit the grapes and joined in the laughter of the other women who were struggling to keep their balance.

Guadalupe began to call out a chant as old as time itself, with a rhythm that harkened back to the most primitive energies. It was the ancient song of the harvest, an invocation of fertility, passion, life itself. The women formed a circle around her, echoing her song as they moved about the vat, pressing the grapes with their feet, following the beat of her chant.

Don Pedro began to clap in perfect counterpoint to their voices. One by one, the men followed his lead, urging the women on in their efforts, clapping out the beat. Then they, too, took up the chant, their deep voices adding resonance to the lilting voices of their wives.

Only Paul held back, the outsider, self-conscious

and embarrassed, yet drawn to the energy and spontaneity. Don Pedro saw his conflict, pulled him over, and handed him a wineskin. Paul took a long drink, and then his inhibitions fell away. Caught up in the fever of the moment and the ancient rhythms, he couldn't tear his gaze away from Victoria . . . her hips swaying to the most primitive of drives, her slender legs dancing in the purple ooze of the crush.

She saw him watching her by the light of the full harvest moon. His clapping spurred her on. She sang to him, gyrating her hips, intensifying his already heightened desires. All around her, the other women danced and clapped and sang to their men.

A year of planting and tending the grapes had ended, the new year about to begin. Guadalupe had performed her rites and given nature its due thanks. The four winds blew their blessing across the valley, bringing good fortune to the extended Aragon family, giving them reason to celebrate through the long harvest night.

Victoria came running into her bedroom, still breathless and laughing with excitement. The ancient fertility ritual had stoked her fantasies, stirring her passion to the boiling point. Her skin burned for Paul's touch. She felt drawn to him like a magnet to a force field . . . his walk, the hungry look in his eyes, his smile. She crossed the room and leaned her elbows on the windowsill, gulping in the night air, quivering with anticipation, the juice of the grapes running down her legs.

The moon hung just beyond her reach—a true harvest moon, orange and heavy against the starlit sky. By tomorrow, it would be on the wane. It would disappear by delicate increments until it was just a wisp, and then nothing at all. But tonight it was hugely present, almost blinding in its brightness, impossible to ignore. She stared at its shadowed surface, thinking that whatever happened tomorrow or the next day after that, tonight she was meant to be with Paul, to make love with him. She couldn't be left wondering for the rest of her life why she had denied herself such pleasure.

He found her there by the window, her skirt hiked up almost to her waist, her brown eyes flashing with desire. The frenzied energy of the ceremony he'd just witnessed had made him half-crazy with passion. He could hardly breathe for wanting her. He stared at her, imagining himself pushing her dress away from her skin, kissing her breasts, making love until they were both sated.

She seemed to float across the space that separated them, and they fell into each other's arms, their mouths locked in a kiss that burned to their very souls. They fell on the bed, their hunger for each other as bottomless as the deepest sea. She whispered his name, and he answered with hers, and then they were past the point of words and language.

Her hands tangled through his hair and coursed down his back. He tore at the buttons on his shirt and tugged at her dress. Her hips rose to meet his, holding nothing back. Her arms were clasped tightly around his neck and she whispered his name over and over again, as if to assure herself it really was he. He tasted the sweetness of her lips, the salt on her skin, the juice of the grapes that had stained her thighs purple.

He drank it all in, caressing her with his hands. And then suddenly, the madness of what they were doing hit him, and he surprised himself by breaking away from her. He sprang up from the bed, leaving them both gasping for air, their bodies aching with thwarted desire.

She lay on the bed, trembling, hugging her arms to her breasts where a moment ago his lips had been. He hated himself, couldn't bear what he was doing to her. Whatever his present feelings might be for Betty, he was still her husband. Come morning, he would have to pack up his things, walk away from *Las Nubes*, and move on.

"I want you more than anything, Victoria," he said, his voice shaking with emotion. "You can't imagine how I want you. But I'm not free, and I won't hurt you that way. I'm sorry . . . I'm so terribly sorry."

She choked back her tears as he stumbled out of the room. She couldn't cry anymore. She had no energy left to go after him and make him understand he couldn't cause her any more pain than she'd already had to bear. She had only strength enough to turn over and stare at the moon for hours. Finally, she fell into a troubled sleep that was haunted by the terrifying image of herself screaming for help as she drowned in a huge vat filled to overflowing with ripe purple grapes.

CHAPTER

· 9 ·

She was up at dawn, awakened by the sun and a sick feeling in her stomach when she thought about the look on Paul's face as he'd rushed out of the room. She didn't know how to think about what had happened between them, except to keep reminding herself that he'd wanted her as badly as she'd wanted him. She glanced out the window, half expecting to see him walking toward the road, his duffel bag slung over his shoulder. But the path was empty, with only a haze of clouds hovering between the house and the mountains beyond.

She quickly undressed and washed herself well, rubbing her legs hard with a soapy sponge to rid them of the purple stains. The bed linens would have to be changed, because they, too, were streaked purple from the grape juice, a bitter reminder of a promise that would never be fulfilled. Determined to put her feelings for Paul behind her, she marched out of her room, her soiled sheets piled under her arm.

She hadn't even reached the stairs when her mother came out of her room, her arms filled with the juice-stained sheets from her bed. And a moment later, they were joined by Guadalupe, who likewise was carrying a bundle of purple sheets.

"Did you have a good night's sleep, *querida*?" Marie Jose teased her daughter.

She and Guadalupe burst out laughing, two gleeful conspirators. Their laughter stopped as Victoria's face darkened with pain. Without saying a word, she ran downstairs, the sheets trailing after her.

Alberto, too, was already awake and moving about the house. After a wonderful night of lovemaking, he would have been in a good mood, except that his son seemed intent on picking a fight with him this morning. Pedro had been following him from room to room, brandishing a journal he'd discovered in his economics class this semester.

"Pop," he said, trailing his father from the kitchen into the hallway, "we can lead the market instead of chasing after it—"

"Where the hell is my hat?" demanded Alberto, whose mind was already focused on the day ahead.

He had no patience for the theories his son's college professors cooked up to impress their students. They were trapped in their ivory towers, totally removed from reality, and could no more understand the business of making money from grapes than they could tell the difference between a pinot noir and a merlot.

"We can raise the money through limited partnerships," Pedro said, beginning to repeat himself.

Alberto was hardly listening as he walked into the parlor, still in search of his missing hat. He found, not the hat, but his daughter's husband, still dressed in the clothes he'd worn the day before. Furthermore, unless Alberto was very much mistaken, the sofa bore the indentation of a man's body. Even Pedro's professors could have figured out that Paul had slept on the parlor sofa, and Victoria had slept alone in Alberto's bed.

"Hi, Paul," said Pedro before Alberto had a chance to question Paul.

Paul got busy rearranging the pillows on the sofa. "Hi, Pedro. Good morning, Mr. Aragon."

"So what do you think, Pop?" said Pedro.

Alberto was still staring at the sofa, trying to figure out what Paul and Victoria were up to. "About what?" he asked distractedly.

"Modernizing the operation." Pedro was getting exasperated. "The limited partnerships."

"You take on a partner, you take on trouble," snapped Alberto, who intended to expand and modernize when hell froze over.

"You can always borrow from the bank," Paul said.

His well-meant suggestion detonated the explosion that had been building since his arrival at *Las*

Nubes. "Listen, just because you harvested a few grapes doesn't give you a say. Stick to your candy, and keep your nose out of our business."

He advanced on Paul, backing him farther and farther against the far wall of the room. "Now, tell me. What is going on here that you sleep one night on the floor, the next on the couch?"

Paul's face reddened. He opened his mouth to respond, but Victoria, who had overheard her father berating Paul, spoke up first from the doorway.

"You'll use any excuse to make him feel unwelcome here, won't you?" she said hotly.

Alberto scowled at her. This was a time for explanations, not excuses, and she was the one who should be making them. "Something is wrong here. This whole thing smells wrong. A girl comes home with a husband nobody ever heard of. With her suitcase as full as when she went away, like she has no place else to go."

"You don't want me here? I'll leave! Is that what you want?" she cried, feeling cornered by the accuracy of his suspicions.

He stared at her, steely-eyed. "I want the truth! That's what I want!" he raged.

"No, you don't. The only truth you want is the truth according to you. That's the only truth you can accept," she shot back, voicing aloud what no one else in the family had ever dared to say to him.

"Try me," he challenged her.

She fought the urge to meet his dare. A certain kind of relief could come of spitting out the truth, of sharing her burden with someone else besides Paul. But the relief would be momentary, because Alberto would instantly turn on her with the full fury of his rage. She wanted Paul to be spared that nightmare. She swallowed her confession and bolted upstairs, with a last despairing glance at Paul before she left.

"The truth is she came home because she loves her family," he said quietly, telling Alberto what he'd learned about Victoria in the very short time he'd known her.

"I told you! Stay out of our business!" Alberto clenched his fists, pushed almost to breaking by his daughter and her candy salesman husband.

His rage was ugly to see, but it paled in comparison to the horrors of the war from which Paul had just returned. "She *is* my business," he said. Then he calmly handed Alberto the hat he'd removed from the sofa the night before. "You were looking for this."

Alberto snatched up his hat and scowled at Paul. The man had brought nothing but trouble into his house. His daughter's story stunk of a lie. She was like her brother, so eager to be Americans that they'd forgotten what was most important in life: their heritage, the grapes, the family. He knew that behind his back they called him an old fool. But they would both see soon enough who was being foolish. He would have the last laugh, or his name was not Alberto Aragon.

A life was growing inside her. Whatever she felt about Tom, about having been with him, she already loved the unborn child they'd conceived together. Even now, plunged into darkest despair because of her fight with her father, she knew that for the sake of the baby, she would have to find a way to make peace with him. If only the truce didn't have to be on his terms, the peace so costly that each time they fought, she felt herself pulling away from him a little more. It wasn't even a question of right or wrong, but rather, his way or no way at all.

She could hear him stomping around downstairs, raging at Paul, shouting at her brother, slamming the door as he left the house. Kneeling by the window in the bedroom, she caught sight of him marching off to the vineyard to nurse his anger. If she was sure of one thing in the world, it was that his love for her was as variable as the outcome of each year's harvest. When the soil and weather conditions were right, the grapes would result in a fine, full-bodied wine. When she behaved "properly," according to his expectations, he would lavish her with affection and approval. If she tried to make her own choices, she would have to live with his rejection.

It wasn't right, she thought, laying her head on her arms. A parent should love a child, no matter what. Her father had taught her to love *Las Nubes*, the valley and the hills and the vines her family had planted there acre by acre, without ever questioning what they meant to her. The land was in her blood;

her blood was in the land. Didn't his children deserve the same unwavering devotion?

That question felt so heavy on her shoulders that when she heard Paul come into the room and call her name, she almost couldn't pick up her head to look at him.

"Victoria." He touched her shoulder.

"What's wrong with me?" Her eyes pleaded with him. She needed answers to her questions so that she could push away the bleakness and move on.

He shook his head. "There's nothing wrong with you," he said, touching her head so softly she might have imagined his hands on her hair.

She whispered the hardest question of all, the one that had plagued her dreams for so long. "I can't even get my own father to love me. How am I ever going to get anyone else to?"

"You will," he said.

"Will I?"

They both knew what she was asking. But it wasn't in his power to give her the response she wanted to hear. Instead, he told her, "The bus leaves in an hour. I'd better get going."

"I'll drive you," she said, pulling herself together.

"No. It's all right. I can walk."

But she needed those few extra minutes with him, to say good-bye away from the house and her family. She pasted on a smile so falsely cheerful that her teeth ached. "He's suspicious enough. How would it look? My husband goes to work, and I don't see him off?" She forced a laugh that almost ended in a sob. "We've fooled them so far."

"Here's the letter."

She unfolded the worn and crumpled note. He'd written his message in a careful, deliberate handwriting, like a schoolboy wanting to impress a teacher who gave extra points for neatness. The letter was just what they'd decided it should be, except for the ending, where he'd taken poetic license and borrowed a line out of Tom's note. " 'I am a free spirit. . . .' " She read the first part of the sentence aloud, but her voice trailed off before she got to the end.

He grimaced. "It sounded cowardly enough when I read it before. I didn't think you'd mind."

"I don't. But you're not a coward," she said. "And I won't have anyone thinking you are." She tore up the letter and threw the pieces in the wastebasket. He was so different from Tom, in every way possible. She would rather take the blame herself than let him take responsibility for Tom's weaknesses.

"Then I'll send a telegram. Saying I died in a car crash. That should do it. Being widowed is more dignified than being abandoned, don't you think?"

She hid her pain by pretending to bend down and retrieve a scrap of paper that had fallen on the floor. "Yes, much more dignified," she said.

He reached his hand out, then abruptly withdrew it.

"I'll get my bags," he said.

The look in his eyes as he left the room told her that if he so much as touched her arm, even for a second, he'd never, ever be able to let her go.

He didn't want to speak to Betty. The very thought made his stomach go queasy. He had nothing to say to her, certainly nothing he could tell her about everything that had happened to him in the last two days. A girl on a train who needed help? A vineyard in the Napa Valley? A grape harvest? He knew what she'd tell him. Time was money, and if he wasn't selling chocolate in Sacramento, he was wasting time *and* money.

He didn't want to hear her say it. But he felt guilty, and hearing her voice might make her seem more real, and when he went to get his jacket from the parlor, the telephone was sitting right there in front of him. She was his wife. He was supposed to call her, right?

He peered out the door to make sure no one was around who might listen in on the conversation. Then he dialed the operator and gave her Betty's number in San Francisco. He thought about all the other times he'd called her, before they were married, to ask her out on a date. He'd get so nervous that she might turn him down that his heart would start to beat too fast, and his hands would get all sweaty. But she'd said yes, every time except once when he was too tired to go out dancing. She'd stamped her foot and said she never wanted to see him again. Of course, she'd changed her mind, and soon after that, they'd decided to get married.

When she didn't answer after three rings, he almost put down the receiver. She was probably already on her way to work. Or maybe she was in the shower. He'd give her one more chance, and then he'd hang up.

She answered on the fourth ring. "Hello?" She seemed distracted, as if he'd pulled her away from something important.

"Betty, it's me," he said.

In the background he thought he heard a man's voice saying something like, "We start from the left. And move our way in. Small fork, first course."

"Paul! I'm so glad you called," she said, sounding as if she really meant it.

"The knife at the top is for the condiments."

The man's voice came through a little more clearly now. He thought he recognized it as that of the very cultured and informative Mr. Knox. Was it another one of his records? Or had the guy started making house calls to his best customers?

"I called Mr. Sweeney to tell him you were back and burning up the tracks, and guess what I wangled out of him?" Her voice rose with excitement.

He imagined her standing by the phone, glancing at one of Armisted Knox's books, maybe even turning the pages as she spoke to him. Her blond curls—if they were still blond—would be bobbing as she prepared to tell him her good news about Mr. Sweeney. Betty certainly was a go-getter. He just wished she'd stop going after what he was supposed to be in charge of getting for himself.

"Six new territories!" she chirped. "All the way to Portland! Starting on this trip you can just keep on going north. Isn't that great?"

"Yeah, great," he said glumly.

He wondered why she seemed so happy to have him out of San Francisco for what could be three or four more weeks. Sure, he could make lots of money with a bigger territory, but didn't she miss him? He'd been away for four years, and now she seemed not to care if he stayed away for four more. "Is someone there?"

"Just Armisted. So are you making millions?"

Armisted the man, or Armisted the record? "Not exactly," he said. "It's a little slow."

"Slow is a word for turtles, Paul Sutton, and you know where the turtle finishes in the race." She giggled, and he remembered how pretty she was. "And remember, sweetie. Time is money."

He almost laughed out loud. She was so predictable. He thought about the story of the turtle and the hare, and realized she had it all wrong. "He won," he said.

"Who won?"

"The turtle. He won the race."

For once, she had nothing to say. Probably Mr. Knox didn't discuss the idea of slow but steady in any of his books or records.

"Betty, what do you think about children?"

There was another long silence. He held his

breath while he waited for her answer. He thought about Victoria's baby, about how he'd always dreamed of being a father so he could give his son or daughter a better life than he'd had.

"Children? How did we get from money to children? Paul, what on earth are you thinking about?"

She reminded him of a teacher he'd had at the orphanage, the one who'd given him a failing mark for writing a story that was too imaginative, not enough about his everyday life.

"I'm thinking about coming home," he said.

This time the silence seemed to stretch on for eternity. He tried to recall what they'd talked about before they got married. Not too much that he could remember. Whether to go eat Chinese or Italian. Whether he liked her new blouse. Whether he agreed with her that Frank Sinatra was much dreamier than Bing Crosby. Whether he loved her the best, more than anyone else in the world.

Her questions had made him laugh and made him feel loved. They were easy to answer, especially the last one. He didn't have anyone else in the world to love.

"Betty?" Maybe the line had gone dead. "Hello?"

But no, she was still there. "Paul, I'm late for an appointment," she said in an oddly cold tone that he hadn't heard before. "I gotta go. 'Bye."

There was a click, and then the hum of the long distance wires. She had hung up on him. He wasn't all that surprised. He wasn't even sure he cared.

* * *

Victoria hadn't meant to eavesdrop on Paul's conversation. It had happened purely by accident, all because she'd asked Pedro if she could borrow his car to drive Paul to the bus, and Pedro thought he'd left his keys in the parlor. She'd gone looking for them and overheard Paul ask the operator to connect him to a San Francisco number. Knowing she was doing something she shouldn't, she'd flattened herself against the wall outside the room and stayed to listen, just for a minute.

He'd never mentioned his wife's name, but she'd concluded that Betty must be his wife. He didn't seem to have much to say to her, which had made Victoria feel unreasonably happy. But her happiness had lasted only a minute, because then she'd heard Paul ask his wife about having children, and then he'd said he was coming home.

Well, why shouldn't he go home? They'd both known all along that he was staying only for a day, two at the most. But hearing him say the words made it real, and the reality had literally stabbed her in the stomach with pain. She'd gasped with shock and grabbed her belly, worried for the baby.

It was such a tiny, fragile entity in her womb, and the pain had been so intense, like a flash of lightning in the summer sky. Lightning could do terrible damage; she'd seen trees split in half by its force, and one of the winery outbuildings had burned to the ground years ago when it had been struck by a bolt during an electrical storm. She needed to protect

herself better to keep from hurting the baby. The
bolt of pain was a warning: No more eavesdropping;
no more yearning after Paul. She simply had to
accept, once and finally, that he was going home to
his wife.

His duffel bag wasn't in the parlor where he'd left
it. Paul checked the upstairs bedroom, the hall, and
even the dining room, but it was not to be found. He
tried to think who might have picked it up by mistake, and then he remembered Guadalupe telling him
yesterday to leave his dirty clothes in the bathroom so
that someone could wash them.

At the orphanage the washing had been done on
the back porch. He hurried to the kitchen and
stepped out the back door. Sure enough, there was
Guadalupe, sorting through a pile of laundry, includ-
ing his dirty uniform which she must have taken
upon herself to remove from his bag. The uniform
wasn't the only item to have come out of the bag. His
silver case lay face-up and open on the ground, so
that Betty's picture was clearly visible to anyone who
walked by.

He couldn't tell whether Guadalupe had seen the
picture, but as she bent down to reach for the case,
he quickly called out to her. *"Senora!"*

He distracted her long enough to scoop up the
case and stick it in his jacket pocket. Then he
pointed to the tub of sudsy water. "I appreciate it
very much. But I don't have time."

"The smell is . . ." Guadalupe held her nose and grimaced.

She was so right. His soiled shirt and pants had taken on the odor of fish that had been left outside to rot beneath a strong sun. "I know. But I have to leave. I have business."

She smiled mischievously. "Don Pedro has finished your business, I think." She gestured to his empty sampler case. "No?"

He laughed, remembering Don Pedro's systematic sampling of his chocolates. Obviously, Guadalupe knew all about her husband's sweet tooth. He wondered whether she'd scolded her husband for eating what he wasn't supposed to, or whether she'd played ignorant and let him have his joke.

"And besides, you must see it through," she said.

"See what through?"

"Your fate." She glanced skyward, then crossed herself. "What brought you here."

"Nothing brought me here. I brought me here."

Guadalupe smiled serenely. Her expression implied that she knew better than he how and why he'd come to *Las Nubes*. She winked at him, picked up his clothes, and dropped them into the washtub. They sank beneath the sudsy water, left to soak there while Guadalupe went back into the house to do her other chores.

This was a plot, he decided, concocted by Don Pedro and Guadalupe to keep him at *Las Nubes*. They meant well, but their good intentions were exasperating and were only likely to make the situation more difficult for Victoria than it already was.

The uniform would have to stay behind. He had a bus to catch. He walked around the house to find Victoria and saw her headed for Pedro's car. Suddenly, she bent over, clutched her stomach, and cried out in pain.

He ran to her and put his arms around her shoulders. "What's wrong?" he asked, worried about the baby.

"Nothing." She shook her head, but the strained look on her face told him otherwise. He glanced around. The yard was empty, the women busy in the house, the men gone off to working the vineyard or the winery.

"Don't say anything. Let me help you upstairs."

She straightened up slowly. Her cheeks were still pale, but her breathing had returned to normal. "No. We had a plan. You were going to stay for one night and go back to your life. We should stick to the plan."

He knew she was right, but she wasn't well. If he walked away from her now, he'd be as bad as Tom, abandoning her when she needed him most. "I can't leave you like this," he said.

"And tomorrow? Will you stay tomorrow, too? And the day after that? Go home, Paul. Like you told your wife you would. Here." She slapped Pedro's car keys into his hand. "Leave it at the station."

"Victoria, please." He held her hand, not wanting her to go.

Maybe Guadalupe was right, and fate had

brought him and Victoria together. But what about Betty? He couldn't simply walk away and disappear from her life. She had hopes and dreams for their future. Why else had she called Mr. Sweeney and persuaded him to increase Paul's territory?

She must have thought he was crazy, phoning out of the blue to ask her if she'd thought about having children. Of course, she wanted kids. What woman didn't? She was just being practical. She wanted them to save some money before they started a family. But he didn't want to have kids with Betty. He wanted to be a father to Victoria's baby.

"Listen to me," he said.

She pulled out of his grasp. "You can't help me anymore, Paul." She shielded her eyes from the sun with her hands and stared at him, as if memorizing his face. "No one can help me," she said and glanced around like a helpless fawn, caught in a hunter's rifle sights without its mother to guide it to safety.

He watched her take off in the direction of the winery and opened his mouth to call her name. But what was the point? She'd say herself that he couldn't give her the help she needed. She'd somehow have to work things out with her family, and he had no place among them.

"Right," he mumbled. "It's not my problem."

He marched back to the porch, retrieved his soaking wet uniform from the tub, and pushed it into his bag.

"Why am I doing this anyway?" he asked himself. He got halfway to Pedro's car before he turned and saw her running into the winery. The answer came from his heart; because he loved her.

"Dammit!" he said.

If four years of staying alive in the jungle had taught him anything, it was that you had to grab your opportunities as they came along. When the stakes were high, you moved as quickly as possible and didn't stop to think about the dangers that might lie hidden in the underbrush.

He dropped his duffel bag and headed over to the winery.

All the while, Guadalupe had been watching him and Victoria through the screen door. He wasn't even halfway across the yard before she came outside, dug into his bag, and retrieved the uniform. Back it went into the soapy water. Fate, in the person of a determined grandmother, had intervened. He wasn't going anywhere on this beautiful September morning, not if Guadalupe had anything to say about it.

From the outside, the winery was just another slate-roofed building covered in masses of ivy. Paul pushed open the heavy wooden door and felt as if he'd stepped into a tomb. The room was cool and damp and silent. He blinked, adjusted his eyes to the dimness after the bright sunshine of the yard, and called out, "Victoria?"

The only sound was a faint trickle of water from somewhere at the back of the building. He moved farther into the room and noticed that the stone walls were lined with racks of bottles laid on their sides, waiting to be corked. Farther in were the wine vats, filled almost to overflowing, and the wine press.

"Victoria!" he called again, searching for her in the narrow walkways between the bottle racks. A cat emerged suddenly from behind the press, startling him with an indignant meow. She brushed her face against his leg, arched her back, then vanished into the darkness.

Victoria was here, hiding somewhere in the shadows, pretending not to hear him call her name. He wondered what words would make her come to him, but he could think of none. Everything she'd said to him was true, yet wasn't there also some deeper truth that sprang from the depths of their feelings for each other? He peered into the dusty corners and wandered among the racks of bottles, each stamped with the *Las Nubes* label and marked according to the type of grape. Cabernet, chardonnay, sauvignon blanc . . . the names were exotic and impossible to pronounce, conjuring up images from a book he'd once read about castles in France.

Alberto was waiting for him when he came round the other side of the racks. He blocked Paul's way, glowering at him through the gloom. "Don't think that just because you married her any of this is yours," he said, pointing to the bottles and vats. He leaned in closer so his face was only inches away from Paul's. "*If* you married her at all."

"What's that supposed to mean?" Paul tried to

edge away from him, but Alberto stepped sideways
and grabbed his arm.

"I wasn't there. I didn't see a wedding. I didn't
even see a wedding certificate," he said. "Don't think
that just because I speak with an accent, I think
with an accent."

His eyes bored into Paul. He looked wild and
fierce, like a warrior who'd prepared himself to do
battle against the enemy. Paul knew that expression.
He'd seen it on the faces of his friends in the jungle.
It frightened him to think that he, too, had learned
how to contort his features so that nothing but the
anger of war was revealed.

"For four years I've been at war," he said, allowing his anger toward Alberto to come spilling out.
"To do what I had to do, I had to keep myself closed
off from feeling anything. What's your reason?"

"What the hell are you talking about? Reason for
what?" Alberto shouted.

"For closing your daughter out of your heart.
Can't you see how amazing she is? How alive?" The
words burst out of him, and as he tried to make
Alberto understand, suddenly he understood the wel-
ter of emotions he'd been struggling with for the last
two days.

"My whole life I've been dreaming of getting the
kind of love your daughter tries to give you," he went
on, speaking more quietly now. "I would die for what
you have. Why can't you just love her? She's so easy
to love."

"You know nothing about my daughter!" Alberto exploded. "You hear me? Nothing!"

"I know that she is good. And strong. And deserves all the love this world has to give. Can't you see that? How wonderful, how special she is?"

Above them, Victoria stood concealed in the shadows of the catwalk that crisscrossed the winery, her tears falling gently as Paul poured out his love for her to her father. Knowing how much he cared lessened the pain of losing him, at least for now. She held her breath, waiting to hear her father's response.

Alberto's expression momentarily softened. Paul sensed that he wanted to let down his guard and accept what Paul was saying. He saw behind Alberto's grim mask a flicker of acceptance. But he couldn't sustain the feeling. The mask fell back into place. The moment passed.

"You see this? This land? This vineyard? This is three hundred sixty-five days a year, twelve hours a day. Year in, year out . . . who do you think I do this for? For them! All of them! Out of love. You don't know what the hell you're talking about! I love my family!"

His voice rang with truth and conviction, and Paul believed him. "Then why don't you let them know?" he said quietly.

This time Alberto didn't try to stop him from leaving. Paul pushed open the winery door and stepped back out into the sunshine.

* * *

Stay or go. Stay or go. The need to decide wracked his brain. He stood in the middle of the yard, closed his eyes, and prayed for Victoria to appear. When he opened his eyes, she was nowhere to be seen. It was fate, he decided, telling him to leave. He picked up his bag and saw that the uniform was missing again. Not unexpectedly, he found it soaking in Guadalupe's tub on the porch. He stuffed the soaking wet clothes back into his bag and headed out of the yard, away from *Las Nubes*.

He was just coming up to the stone-walled cave where the wine was stored to be aged when he noticed Don Pedro standing just outside the entrance, chatting with his three chief assistants. Behind them were two of the vineyard carts, stacked high with the oak barrels that held the newly pressed wine.

"Paul!" Don Pedro waved him over.

His chances of making the bus were fast fading. But he couldn't ignore Victoria's grandfather, who'd treated him so warmly from the first moment of his arrival. He ducked under the low ceiling of the entrance to the cave and joined Don Pedro, who had just finished eating what looked to have been a prodigious amount of food. A chunk of cheese, a heel of bread, and a slice of spicy sausage were all that remained on his plate.

The three men went back to work, unloading the barrels and rolling them into the cave, and Don Pedro pulled Paul down next to him onto the low stone bench where he'd been sitting. He held up a bottle, dusty with age, and pointed proudly to its label.

"Brandy," he said. "The finest." He poured a glass and handed it to Paul. "I made it myself, twenty-one years ago."

Paul had never tasted brandy and wasn't especially eager to do so now. But refusing even to taste it would be an insult to the winegrower. He took a sip and winced at its sharpness. His lips and tongue stung as he swallowed.

Don Pedro chuckled. "The secret to brandy is age. The secret to everything is age," he said.

He poured a glass for himself and downed it in one long gulp. Grinning broadly, he motioned to Paul to do likewise.

The wise thing would have been to say no, thank you, and leave. Paul stared out the door at the road that led over the hill and away from the Aragons. Once he started down the other side of that hill, Victoria, Don Pedro, this valley would be lost to him forever. Mr. Sweeney's chocolates were no match for the magic and beauty he'd found at *Las Nubes*.

One glass, he decided. Out of courtesy to Don Pedro, his host.

He smiled at Don Pedro, steeled himself, and gulped down the brandy. He felt the alcohol before he tasted it, its liquid heat spreading quickly from his mouth to his stomach to his limbs.

Don Pedro bent down and trailed his hand through the thin trickle of water dripping from Paul's duffel bag. He threw back is head and roared with laughter. "Newlyweds." He shook his head. "What else do they do but make love and war? Did you talk to her?"

Paul wished his problems with Victoria really were as simple as the lovers' spat Don Pedro misunderstood it to be. "I tried," he said with a shrug.

"It wouldn't make a difference anyway," said Don Pedro, pouring himself another glass. "Talking between men and women never solves anything. Where we think, they feel. They are creatures of the heart."

He tapped his heart with the brandy bottle and refilled Paul's glass. "I have the perfect solution. Salud!" He drained his glass, then wiped his mouth with the back of his hand.

Could Don Pedro truly find a way for him and Victoria to share a life together? His head spinning from the alcohol, Paul was almost ready to believe that the unthinkable could be made possible. He tipped his glass to Don Pedro and smiled crookedly.

"Salud!" he said. "To the perfect solution!"

CHAPTER

· 10 ·

Every September, it was the happy duty of Father Filippo Coturri, the priest at the church where Victoria and Pedro had been baptized, to supervise the preparations for the harvest festival. Because he himself had grown up on a farm, he understood and valued the importance of the harvest to his parishioners. It was a time to give thanks, to appreciate the bounties that the good Lord had seen fit to bestow on His faithful servants. It was a time to take stock, renew old friendships, find a match for an eligible son or daughter among the other valley families. Above all, it was a time to celebrate.

There was much to do on the day preceding the festival. The banner announcing the festival had to be hung across the plaza in the middle of town. A stage had to be constructed in the plaza from the redwood planks that were stored the rest of the year in the church basement. There were decorations to be made, flowers to be gathered and arranged. No preharvest preparation was complete without the inevitable crisis: The billowy yellow cloth that hung above the stage to block the sun was missing from the rectory closet; the tablecloths were torn or creased or stained from last year's spilled wine; rain was predicted, though rain hadn't fallen in September in the valley for as long as anyone could remember.

Father Filippo, who was white-haired and seldom stopped smiling, stood back to inspect the banner, which had just been hammered into place by two of the townsfolk. He rubbed his hands in gleeful anticipation. The crises would pass. The sun would shine. The festival would be the most wonderful ever in the history of the valley.

At *Las Nubes*, the Aragons were also immersed in preparations for the festival. Alberto and Pedro, along with several of their workers, were grooming their prize stallions upon whose backs they would triumphantly ride into town. Later, they would clean and wax their saddles, and polish the silver bits on the bridles. Pedro had been helping his father with these jobs since he was a little boy. It was a ritual both father and son enjoyed, and in recent years, it was one of the few occasions when they didn't argue.

The women had gathered in the kitchen to iron the elaborate costumes of the *charros*, the Mexican cowboys, which they would all be wearing to the festival. Each piece of the costume—shirt, jacket, shawl, pants—had to be inspected for rips or moth holes, and mended, if necessary. The task was time-consuming and tiring, but it was done with much love and laughter.

Guadalupe and Marie Jose, Maria and Consuela, all of them chatted cheerfully as they worked around the table. Only Victoria was quiet, her head bent over a shirt that had been missing a button. She couldn't get out of her mind the image of Paul leaving the winery and walking out of her life. When she reached for her thimble, Marie Jose saw the tears running silently down her cheeks.

"He just went to work," she said, touched by her daughter's devotion to Paul. "He will come back."

Her words, meant to be consoling, were like acid splashed across an open wound. The pain was excruciating. Victoria bolted out of the room and up the stairs to her parents' bedroom. She shut the door behind her, sat down on the bed she had shared with Paul, and stared bleakly at the rose, now wilted and fading, that her mother had left on the pillow only two nights earlier. She held it to her breasts and went to the window. The harvested vineyard, stripped bare of its fruit, looked colorless and sad.

She heard a knock at the door, and then her mother asked, "Victoria, are you all right?"

"Yes, Mama," she said.

Come next summer, the grapes would be ripening again on the vines. Her baby would be born before then. Life would go on, but it would never be the same for her without him.

* * *

All afternoon Don Pedro's assistants carted oak barrels into the cave and stacked them one on top of each other to the height of the low wood-beamed ceiling. In between loads they would traipse back to the dark recesses of the cave where Don Pedro had settled down to teach Paul an old Mexican love song. The "perfect solution" he had proposed was for Paul, accompanied by himself and the assistants, to serenade Victoria with the song after she went to bed that evening.

The music lesson was going badly. When Don Pedro sang the melody, it was lilting and romantic. The Spanish words flowed off his tongue like poetry. But in Paul's mouth the same words sounded raucous and harsh, and the melody got twisted into unfamiliar shapes. Don Pedro refused to become discouraged. He had seen the love in his granddaughter's eyes whenever she looked at her young man. He would have moved mountains if he thought that was what it would take to reconcile them. But he'd sung this same song beneath Guadalupe's window when he'd courted her, and he was sure it would have the same effect on Victoria as it had had on her grandmother.

Frequent and liberal doses of brandy sustained his good spirits. His optimism was contagious, as was his thirst. Paul kept matching him glass for glass. But the alcohol didn't seem to improve his voice or his Spanish accent.

"You're a gringo," said Don Pedro, pouring another round from the apparently bottomless bottle. "A nice one, but still a gringo. The heart you talk to is pure Mexican. You must speak to it in a language it understands. Be strong."

Paul had thought he was being strong when he sang, but maybe he was just being loud. It was possible that his judgment was being affected by the brandy, although he was quickly getting used to the taste. Its warmth radiated throughout his body, creating a wonderful glow that extended into the room itself. San Francisco seemed a million miles away, Betty a distant memory of a woman he'd known only briefly. As Don Pedro filled his glass yet again, he could almost begin to believe it was indeed a lover's quarrel that had caused the rift with Victoria.

The rehearsal in the cave went on through dinner, which consisted of more cheese and sausage as well as chocolate from Don Pedro's secret stash, and continued until nightfall. Eventually, Don Pedro decided it was time for the show to begin. His soloist was as prepared as he would ever be. His three assistants, who would accompany Paul on two guitars and a harp, were ready, as well. Their instruments in hand, they trooped up to the house behind Paul and Don Pedro, who was armed with the last of the brandy.

Except for a light on the porch, the house was dark. Don Pedro led his band of musicians to the lawn directly below Victoria's window and arranged them so that Paul was standing in front, the three others just slightly behind him.

That done, Don Pedro retreated to a spot beneath the eaves of the porch and treated himself to another shot of brandy. Then, with a wave of his hand, he signaled for the music to begin.

They started slowly, their instruments murmuring the opening chords. As Paul waited for his cue, a sudden flash of clarity shone through his brandy-induced haze, and he saw the foolishness of Don Pedro's scheme. He'd been miscast in the role of a Spanish-speaking Romeo to Victoria's Juliet. They were star-crossed lovers; that much was true. But he had no business being here. Victoria had made it very clear that she wanted nothing more to do with him, and his mangled version of a Mexican love song was not what he wanted her to remember him for.

He looked over at Don Pedro, who motioned to him to join in with the other musicians, as they'd rehearsed it. Paul shook his head, no. Don Pedro waved the brandy bottle and nodded, yes, do it. Paul opened his mouth, but nothing came out. The words weren't there. His voice was frozen in his throat.

"Be strong," Don Pedro whispered a reminder.

Paul swallowed his doubts and tried to sing the song just as Don Pedro had instructed him to. Behind him, the assistants gradually increased their volume. The melody of love floated through the night and danced toward the moon.

Victoria, who was still awake, heard it first. The music wafting through her window made her wonder whether she'd gone mad with grief. How else to explain this hallucination of a moonlight serenade?

Marie Jose was the next to be touched by the music, which pulled her out of a deep sleep and went straight to her heart. She sat up in bed and strained to hear the sounds that had penetrated her dreams. She heard guitars, a harp, someone singing the most familiar of love songs. The music was haunting, heartbreakingly beautiful.

"Alberto," she whispered and gently shook her husband awake.

He stirred and moved over to hold her, breathing to the slow, measured tempo of the song.

Pedro was reading in his bedroom when the music made him look up from his economics textbook. He lay back against his pillows and thought about the blue-eyed girl who sat next to him in sociology and whether she liked to ride and how she'd feel about living so far from the city.

Guadalupe had sneaked out to the cave to find her errant husband. This evening hadn't been the first time he'd missed dinner, and it wouldn't be the last. She understood that sometimes he needed to go off by himself, to indulge his appetite for all the foods that were forbidden him.

She surveyed the remains of his illicit feast and smiled indulgently, loving him now as much and more as she'd loved him when they'd met. She began to clean up the mess he'd left behind, and then she, too, heard the music. She stopped to listen and smiled again, transported across more than fifty years of marriage, to a village in Mexico where a young man stood outside her father's house and serenaded her in the darkness.

Don Pedro helped himself to another brandy and hummed the melody as the musicians played on and Paul grew ever more uncomfortable.

The hallucination felt so real that Victoria was drawn out of bed and over to the window. Her heart was pounding as she peeked through the curtain, and what she saw only confused her more. She couldn't make sense of why and how Paul had come to be standing out there on the grass, serenading her in Spanish.

"No," she said, though what she really meant was yes.

"Remember," Don Pedro called to Paul. "Look for the light. When she turns it on, you are saved!"

The assistants were playing as if they'd been born to be musicians and reared as a trio. They were singing now, as well, giving voice to harmonies as rich and sweet as nectar. It was the joy they took from singing that made Paul realize he'd blundered into someone else's song. He looked for the light, as Don Pedro had said to. Victoria's window was dark, the room within hidden behind a curtain that fluttered in the breeze. For her peace of mind and his, he couldn't spend another night at *Las Nubes*.

The song was reaching its climax. Marie Jose nestled into Alberto's arm and turned her face up to receive his kisses. He stroked her arm and touched her lips with his fingertips.

"I tell you one thing," he said softly. "He tries very hard. He seems to love her. Maybe I have been too tough on him. Maybe it is time to make peace."

"Alberto," she whispered.

He smiled at her through the darkness. "It was a good serenade."

"Yours were better," she murmured as her lips met his.

The music was drawing to a passion-filled conclusion. Alone in her room, Victoria fought a battle between her heart and her head. She reached to turn on the lamp, then pulled back her hand as if she'd touched it to a hot stove. She couldn't call him to her. She knew Paul loved her, because she'd heard him say so to her father. But he'd told Betty he was coming home. She had to let him go.

Finally, he was leaving. He picked up his bag and walked away from Don Pedro and the three assistants. The last stirrings of the serenade lingered in the air as he followed the road past the winery, past the cave, and started climbing the hill that would take him to the other side of the valley.

The song was done. The assistants put down their instruments. Don Pedro swallowed the last of the brandy. His idea had failed. There was no perfect solution for his granddaughter. Feeling old and defeated, he walked into the house and went to find his wife.

Paul reached the top of the hill just as the numbing effects of the brandy were beginning to wear off. He could feel a pounding headache creeping up the base of his neck and across the top of his scalp. Though the night was balmy, he shivered as he took the next-to-final step that would put *Las Nubes* out of sight forever. He stared at the road below him where he'd encountered Victoria, weeping as she sat enthroned atop her suitcase. He'd learned so much since then, painful lessons but nevertheless valuable ones.

He turned to take one last look and found the sign that he'd been hoping for. A light was shining in Victoria's room. Don Pedro would have said he was saved and pushed him up the stairs to claim his wife. Don Pedro, however, knew only the better half of the truth, which was that he and Victoria were very much in love. He couldn't go back now, as much as he might want to. His wife was waiting for him. Feeling all alone in the world, he began to make his way down the hill and disappeared into the night.

CHAPTER

· 11 ·

Bright sunshine and a crystal blue sky showed the valley off in all its most glorious mid-September splendor. Father Filippo beamed with the pleasure of a man who knew that his prayers had been answered and all was right in his most beautiful corner of the world. The ladies of the Harvest Festival Committee had been up since dawn putting the finishing touches on the decorations for the stage. They'd surely outdone themselves for this first harvest after the war, when there was extra cause to give thanks for peace and on behalf of all the young men who'd returned in safety to their families.

Though it was still early in the day, the plaza was already packed with townspeople and winegrowers from vineyards throughout the valley. Their names and accents reflected the international flavor of the community. As was traditional, they'd come in their distinctive native costumes: the Swiss wore peaked feathered hats; the Hungarians had on intricately embroidered vests; the Italians, who constituted the largest number in the group, sported colorful peasant shirts and long skirts for the women. And in this year of peace, even the Germans had seen fit to wear their suspendered lederhosen and matching leather caps.

From his place of honor on the stage Father Filippo presided happily over his flock. The long table in front of him held their symbolic thanksgiving offerings—prized bottles of wine and fat bunches of grapes, the first cut from the vines, arranged in straw baskets of various sizes. Soon he would recite the blessing of the harvest, thanking God for the bountiful season just passed, and praying for a successful year to come. He only had to await the arrival of the Aragons, for Don Pedro was recognized as among the preeminent vintners in the valley.

The festival had hardly begun, but already the noise in the plaza was loud enough to attract the attention of the soldiers who'd spent the night at the USO dormitory just at the edge of the plaza. Most of the men and women lodged there were just passing through town and had no idea what all the fuss was about. The celebration was a picturesque novelty that momentarily grabbed their interest before they moved on to their final destinations.

The most curious had gathered at the window that overlooked the square. Paul stood among them, dressed in his somewhat wrinkled but otherwise clean uniform, and wistfully watched the goings-on, wishing he were there among the celebrants.

"Bus leaves for San Francisco in ten minutes!" the receptionist announced.

His bus. He was about to move away from the window when another announcement caught his ear. "The Aragons! The Aragons are coming!" He stood rooted to the spot, hoping to catch even one quick glimpse of Victoria and the family he'd begun to think of as his own.

Below him on the plaza, all heads turned and looked toward the far end of the street. A buzz of excitement passed through the square. The Aragons were famous for arriving in grand style, and their advent into the plaza today was no exception.

As always, they all were dressed in the costume of the *charros*, their heads held high beneath their hugely wide-brimmed straw hats. Don Pedro rode at the head of the procession on a magnificent jet black stallion, and Alberto and Pedro followed just behind him. The gold braid of their jackets and pants glittered in the sunlight as their horses high-stepped through the cobblestoned street. The women came next, riding sidesaddle on snowy white mares. Behind them came Don Pedro's three assistants, the erstwhile musicians, and next in line, their families on a flatbed pulled by two large dray horses.

The crowd applauded enthusiastically at the spectacle. Don Pedro and Alberto held their heads up high and seemed to take no notice, while Guadalupe and Marie Jose played their parts and waved to their friends in the crowd. Victoria, who had never looked prettier, couldn't even manage a smile.

She had pleaded with her mother to let her stay home, but of course, that was unthinkable. No one could miss the festival, unless . . . Marie Jose probed delicately . . . was she not well? Was there some special piece of news, to be shared for the time being only with her mother? She'd brushed Victoria's hair away from her forehead and held her breath, hoping for the joyous confirmation that would explain her daughter's constant tears, her paleness, her moodiness. Victoria had turned her head away in shame and pretended not to understand her mother's hints. She longed to tell her mother the truth. But that would only lead to more lies, or worse, utterly ruin the day for her and the rest of the family.

She dutifully put on her costume and combed her hair and mounted her horse. But the ride into town had seemed interminable, and she'd hardly responded to anything her mother or grandmother had asked her. Now, as Don Pedro led them through the throng, she stared listlessly ahead, her eyes fixed on a point in the distance where her thoughts could safely turn to Paul.

Because she couldn't stop thinking about him, he was everywhere . . . here in the plaza, right in front of her. But no . . . she wasn't imagining things. It really was Paul, his eyes locked onto hers, gazing steadily at her until she rode past him, and then he was lost in the crowd.

* * *

Don Pedro rode on, mindful only of the crowd's high spirits and his own elation over the promise of this year's excellent vintage. The love song played itself in his head, and he remembered Guadalupe's face when he'd knelt before her naked in their bed. He moved forward to the stage, where the sight of Father Filippo immediately banished such carnal thoughts and brought him back to the present.

He held up his hand and his family drew to a halt. They dismounted their horses and followed him up onto the stage, standing in silence as he presented the priest with the first bunch of grapes that had been cut from the vines and a prize bottle of wine.

The two men were old friends who had drunk many a glass of wine together. Father Filippo beamed at him, then motioned for those assembled to be quiet. "I will now recite the blessing of the harvest," he announced.

The crowd went silent. Paul watched from the back of the plaza as the priest recited, "We thank You, Lord in heaven, for bestowing on us the bounty of Thy harvest. We ask only that each life here be blessed with the full measure of love, health, and happiness that those who acknowledge God in heaven justly deserve. Amen."

"Amen!" echoed his parishioners.

Father Filippo held up the bottle that Don Pedro had presented to him, uncorked it, and poured the wine into a silver chalice. He held the chalice aloft so that even those standing at the edge of the plaza could be part of the ceremony.

"Bless this wine," he prayed, "the product of the harvest that You have given us."

Still holding the cup high, he sniffed the bouquet, took a sip, and swished it around in his mouth like the true connoisseur that he was after serving for so many decades in the Napa Valley. He smiled his approval and swallowed the wine.

"Excellent!" he declared.

A cheer went up around him, and the crowd surged forward. Dozens of eager winegrowers reached over to uncork the bottles on the stage and hand them around. The women quickly produced glasses, and wine was poured round. Moments later, everyone seemed to be toasting and drinking to one another's good health and happiness. Soon they would unpack the picnic baskets and the food would be laid out on blankets wherever they could find room. Now, however, it was time to taste the wine. The party had begun.

Paul lingered until the very last minute, thinking he might catch sight again of Victoria. When the bus pulled into the depot next to the USO dormitory, he reluctantly pulled himself away from the plaza and stepped over the curb to the street.

"Your serenade was beautiful." The voice that spoke to him was one he'd thought he'd never hear again. He turned around to look at Victoria.

"Will you toast with me?" she asked, offering

him a glass filled with wine that was the color of rubies.

"What do we toast to?" he asked, overwhelmed by her beauty and her sadness.

Tears gleamed in her eyes. "To . . . what if . . ." she murmured.

They touched their glasses to each other's and sipped the wine. His eyes never left her face as they slowly drained the glasses. The bus would be leaving any minute. But first they had to complete the toast by finishing their wine.

Paul raised his glass again and suddenly felt a hand clamp down on his shoulder. Behind him was Alberto, smiling as if he were actually pleased to see him, accompanied by the priest who had blessed the grapes.

"Father Fillipo," said Alberto. "May I introduce Paul Sutton, my new son-in-law." He pointed to the medals on Paul's shirt. "As you can see, a bona fide war hero. He helped bring in the harvest."

Paul and Victoria were too stunned by Alberto's wholly unexpected reversal to do anything but stare at him in openmouthed silence.

Victoria recovered first. "Papa!" she exclaimed.

"What?" He chuckled. "Can't I be proud?"

She glared at him. As usual, he had come around too late, on his terms and only when it suited him. Paul stared over his shoulder at the bus to San Francisco, now departing from the depot.

Ignorant of the drama unfolding before him, Father Fillipo was quite simply and purely delighted by the news. "This is a blessed surprise. Congratulations, Victoria!"

"Thank you, Father," she said weakly.

"I gave her First Communion," Father Fillipo told Paul. "I always thought I'd give her in marriage."

"And you shall." Alberto clapped Paul on the back. "City Hall is not a proper place to take your wedding vows. Not for my only daughter." He put his hands on either side of his mouth and hallooed above the confusion in the plaza. When the noise subsided somewhat, he bellowed at the crowd, "Tonight I give my daughter's hand in marriage before the eyes of God. And I will take it as a personal insult if you all do not show up. You are all invited!"

A roar went up among the revelers. More wine was poured, and another round of toasts began, in honor of the young couple.

"Why are you doing this?" Victoria demanded as Father Filippo went off to sample another bottle.

Alberto chuckled. He was a happy man today. All his hard work of the last year had paid off. The grapes were as sweet and abundant as any he could remember. He loved his wife, and he wished his daughter the same joy in life that he'd found with Marie Jose. Her young man had proven himself to be a hard worker. Perhaps, in time, he might even become less of an outsider.

"A man can change his mind, can't he?" he cheerfully answered Victoria's question.

Before she could say anything else, he was

whisked away by some of his well-wishing friends for more toasting and congratulations.

Paul and Victoria stared at each other. "We have to tell them," he said.

She shook her head. "*I* have to tell them. I can't let you go through this for me any longer. I'm not scared now. If they don't love me"—she touched her stomach—"love *us*, that's their loss. Someone will. I know that now."

She smiled faintly and brushed her hand across his, her eyes expressing so much more than her words.

"Here." He pulled one of the medals off his shirt and handed it to her. "For the baby. A little present."

She stroked the metal bar. "What did you get it for?"

"Courage under fire," he said. He closed her hand over it and clenched his fist over hers.

They stood their together, alone in the middle of so many people, not speaking, hardly even breathing, each thinking the other's thoughts.

"Victoria!" Marie Jose shouted across the plaza.

Victoria tore her gaze away from Paul and looked over at her mother, who was surrounded by a group of her friends, obviously eager to make a fuss over the new bride. She was waving her arms and calling, "Victoria!"

"I'd better get this over with," Victoria said. But she couldn't move. Tearing herself away from him was tantamount to tearing out her heart.

"Paul Sutton, you are the most honorable man I have ever known," she whispered.

She threw her arms around him and kissed him fiercely, a long, deep kiss filled with all the passion that had been locked up inside her. It was a gift to herself and to him, for helping her find the courage to put behind the fears of her childhood. And for remembrance.

Then just as abruptly as she'd kissed him, she broke away and ran to find her family.

Telling them was easier and more difficult than she'd imagined. The hardest part was getting them to stop chattering on about all the things that would have to be done by the evening, so that they could put on a proper wedding. They were all so thrilled by Alberto's decision that no one would listen to her announcement that there wasn't going to be any wedding.

Marie Jose and Guadalupe were too busy whispering to each other that they'd known Alberto would relent. Don Pedro was boasting to his grandson that he deserved all the credit for the wedding, because without his help, the lovers would still be at odds. Alberto was basking in the glory of his decision and collecting good wishes from everyone who passed by.

Victoria burst into tears, which at least got them to pay attention to her. Marie Jose clucked sympathetically about pre-wedding jitters and said she'd been so nervous the day before her wedding that she'd almost called it off. Alberto snorted skeptically and said *he* remembered things differently, at which point Victoria almost despaired of ever making her confession.

Finally, she said in a very small voice that she had something important to tell them, and please, couldn't they be quiet, just for a minute? All around them people were dancing and laughing and eating and drinking. Her family was staring at her elatedly. There was nothing for her to do but say it, that she was sorry, more sorry than they could ever know, but she was pregnant and Paul wasn't the father and she couldn't marry him because he was already married to somebody else.

She made herself look at each one of them in turn. Yes, she was ashamed and worse than that, she hated herself for disappointing them. But for the sake of the baby she was carrying, she wasn't going to walk through the rest of her life hanging her head in shame.

Marie Jose was the first to break the shocked silence. She'd known since the second Victoria had walked through the door that something was amiss. If she were honest with herself, she would have to admit that she'd even known her daughter was pregnant. A mother sensed such things. There would be time enough later to ask questions and hear the whole story. Her baby was in pain. She folded Victoria into her arms and murmured soft, soothing noises, rocking back and forth as she used to do when her children were little.

The rest of the family quickly followed Marie Jose's example. Whatever mistakes she'd made, she was still their beloved Victoria. And there was a child to think about—a new generation of Aragon. Don Pedro, Guadalupe, Pedro, Jr., all rallied around her alongside Marie Jose in a tight little circle of love and forgiveness. They all wept with her and held her hands and begged her not to cry because everything would work out fine.

All except Alberto, who stood apart from them and couldn't look past his own pain to understand hers. His daughter had betrayed him. She had taken their pride and selfishly mangled it to shreds. He looked around the plaza at all his friends and neighbors, who were expecting his daughter to be married in the evening. The name of Aragon had always and only been spoken of with respect. They were people of honor, who knew how to behave themselves. But not anymore. His daughter had made a mockery of his heritage. He could never forgive her for betraying the family.

At the time, trying to hitch a ride instead of waiting hours for the next bus had seemed like a smart idea. By late afternoon Paul wasn't so sure. He'd started walking because, for both their sakes, he needed to put distance between himself and Victoria. But there wasn't much traffic coming by on the road out of town, and the duffel bag was getting heavier and more cumbersome with each mile. Another bus was due to come by in an hour or so. In the meantime he kept plodding along, hoping that his uniform would persuade someone to stop and pick him up.

The sun had started to slide behind the mountains, and the sky was getting pinker now. Just twenty-four hours ago, he'd watched Guadalupe invoke the four winds. He thought of her, standing among the grapes in the middle of the vat, and he made himself stop thinking, before his mind drifted back to Victoria.

Looking around, it hit him suddenly that he'd reached the same place in the road where she'd showed him Tom's letter and told him about the baby. He stopped to rest a moment and stared up the dirt road that sloped over the hill to *Las Nubes*. Homesickness—the fact of missing a place, a house, physical surroundings—was something he'd never understood before. But his longing to climb the hill so he could see the vineyards floating in the valley below was so intense that he almost started up the path.

As if by divine intervention, a truck roared up the road heading south. He quickly stuck out his thumb and was relieved to see the driver pull to a stop just short of him.

"Where are you headed?" asked the driver.

"San Francisco," said Paul.

The driver nodded. "I'll get you as far as San Rafael."

That would get him more than halfway there. He

climbed up into the cab and stowed his bag under the seat.

"What you been doing up here?" the driver asked.

He almost laughed out loud. It would take him all the way to Mexico and then some to answer the question. He gave the simplest response he could think of. "Walking . . . in the clouds," he said, staring up the road as the driver shifted into gear.

The driver glanced at him, decided he must be kidding, and chuckled. "Well, welcome back to earth," he said.

He was exhausted beyond imagining, weary of the jungle, of the endless skirmishes and battles. He'd returned to the orphanage, to check for survivors. What was the point? The place had been bombed almost to smithereens. No one could have been left alive in there. He was still trying to make himself go inside when the door opened and a young woman walked outside. It was Victoria, and she was holding the hand of a little boy, dressed in a uniform that was several sizes too big for him. Victoria! She was still alive! His fatigue gone, he ran to her, but before he even reached the porch, the door slammed shut, and she disappeared.

He bolted up the stairs and flung open the door. There was a deafening blast of noise, followed by a flash of light as bright and hot as the center of the sun. A wind like a hurricane roared past him. The space on the other side of the door went black, and the mushroom cloud of an atomic explosion exploded in a hideous spectrum of colors too vivid to be real.

He woke up gasping and realized he'd been dreaming again, always the same dream about the orphanage in the jungle, and the little boy whom he could never reach in time. In time for what? he wondered. He stared out the window of the truck into the darkness of the night, seeing nothing but the stars twinkling overhead and the moon, already starting to lose its fullness. And then he remembered the woman in the dream, that she'd been Victoria, and that he'd lost her, too.

San Francisco at sunrise was quiet and empty. Paul heard his footsteps echoing in the stillness as he walked up the winding street to Betty's building. When he got to the door, he took out the case that held his keys and with them, Betty's picture. He stared at it in the pale dawn light, studying her features, trying to make himself believe that he loved her. And if he didn't? he wondered, as he climbed the stairs to the third floor. Could love fall away so easily, like a leaf from a tree in autumn? Had he ever loved her?

He tiptoed into the apartment. The morning light had barely pierced the drawn shades, but there was light enough to see that the letters he'd sent from overseas were spread out on the kitchen table. Betty had taken most of them out of the envelopes, and the pages were strewn about, as if she'd systematically gone through them, reading them, at last.

"Who's there?" she said drowsily from the bedroom.

"It's me," he said.

She appeared in the doorway a few seconds later, tousled with sleep, pulling on a bathrobe over her naked body.

He pointed to the letters. "You read them," he said.

She looked at him oddly, as if she weren't quite sure what he was doing there. "Yes." She nodded and tightened the sash on her robe. "Paul," she said, stifling a yawn. "I—"

She was interrupted by a man's voice coming from the bedroom. "Betty?"

Paul stared at her, and she looked beyond him, pursing her lips. He started walking toward the bedroom, but she put out a hand to stop him. "Paul," she said, speaking in a rush. "It wasn't going to work, for either of us. If I had just read the letters sooner . . ." She shrugged. "We hardly knew each other. We want different things, different lives."

He was too stunned to speak. Before he could collect his thoughts, the man called out again, "Who is it, Betty?"

It was all a bad joke. He'd walked away from the best woman he'd ever meet, come all this way to prove that he could be a good, faithful husband, willing to try to make the marriage work . . . only to discover that she was already so sure they didn't

belong together that she'd taken up with someone
else.

"I don't even like dogs," she wailed as he moved
by her to the bedroom.

A naked man jumped out of her bed. The man
reached for the first thing he could find to cover his
bare crotch—and came up with the jacket from
Betty's Armisted Knox record. Paul blinked, wondering whether he was still dreaming. He glanced from
the picture of Armisted Knox on the record jacket to
the man's face, and realized that they were one
and the same person.

"It's not what it appears to be," Armisted Knox
said nervously.

He shook his head, not quite believing what he
was seeing. "Armisted?"

Knox backed away from Paul and grabbed for
his clothes.

Betty moved over to stand between him and
Knox. "Paul, please, listen to me," she said deter-
minedly. "What we want is so opposite. It would
never have worked for me."

She had fairly well summed up what he'd been
thinking about himself. But it was all too much to
take in. He'd thought they could try and make a go
of things. Wasn't that how it was supposed to work?
It hadn't occurred to him that they could just snap
their fingers and make their marriage go away.

"I would have been miserable," she said.

Suddenly, he was very angry. "I came all the way
back here—"

"You don't have a gun, do you?" asked Armisted Knox, frantically trying to pull on his pants.

Paul glared at Betty. She could at least have discussed it with him before deciding to give up and throw him away like yesterday's newspaper. "I was ready to try." Furious with her for not wanting to do even that much, he picked up one of Knox's shoes and threw it against the wall.

"Paul, don't do anything crazy," she warned.

"I'll leave," Knox assured him. "I'll just get my things." He tried to squeeze past Paul to get to the door. Without thinking about what he was doing or why, Paul grabbed his arm. "Don't hit me!" Knox shouted, terrified.

No, of course not. He shook his head. "I'm not going to hit you." He let go of Knox's arm, and Knox streaked out the door, still naked, with his clothes bundled under his arm.

He still felt very confused and uncertain about what was happening here. What about *love*? he wanted to ask her. What about all the promises they'd made, and the good times they'd shared? He wasn't a pair of pants, to be tried on and returned to the store because the fit wasn't right.

"Betty." He cast about for a way to explain his feelings.

She took a piece of paper out of her drawer and handed it to him. "Paul, we can still be friends," she said.

"Friends?"

"I thought an annulment would be the easiest."

She pointed to a blank line on the bottom of the page. "You just have to sign it."

He tried to read the words of the document, but he couldn't seem to focus his eyes. When had she applied for an annulment? Was it the same day she called George Sweeney to get him a bigger sales territory? She didn't want to be his wife anymore. He would be alone again, without a family, without a home. Things were happening too quickly.

"Paul, I'm sorry," she said quietly.

He believed her, but sorry didn't make him feel any better.

In his haste to flee the scene, Armisted Knox had left the door wide open. Paul picked up his bag and walked out without bothering to say another word, not even good-bye. He walked down the stairs, wondering what to do next. He had a little money saved up, enough that if he wanted to take a couple of weeks off before going back to work, he would probably be okay. If he was really careful, he could even quit his job and use the time to look for a new one. He'd have to find a place to stay.

But as long as he went along with the annulment, nobody had any claims on him. He could do whatever he wanted. The whole range of possibilities suddenly spread themselves out in front of him, as vast and limitless as the midwestern prairies of his childhood.

"Paul." Betty leaned out the window of her apartment. "Paul? Are you okay?" she asked.

He filled his lungs with the fresh morning air blowing in from the ocean. It couldn't have worked out for them, but he never would have admitted that they'd made a mistake. He would have stuck around, miserably trying to make the best of a bad situation, instead of facing up to the truth. Maybe Betty had taught him a good lesson this morning. Bravery under fire took lots of different shapes.

"Yeah, I'm fine." He smiled up at her.

She didn't even like dogs. Well, why didn't she say so before they got married?

He thought he saw a trace of regret in her eyes, or maybe it was just her eagerness to get back into bed with Armisted Knox. "See ya'," she said.

He waved the annulment papers at her, his reprieve from a life sentence in solitary confinement, and took off down the hill, whistling as he watched the sun rise. With any luck he could get to *Las Nubes* by dawn. No, he corrected himself. It wasn't a question of luck. It was fate.

CHAPTER

· 12 ·

There was a natural cycle to life at *Las Nubes* that was dictated by the growing season of the grapevines and was far more powerful than the personal well-being of any one member of the family. Once the grapes were harvested, the vines had to be tended to, protected from the winter frosts that could stunt or kill them. Normally, Alberto was in charge of putting the vineyard to sleep for the winter—repairing the irrigation lines, pruning the vines, burning the cane-wood that was collected, weeding the yellow mustard flowers whose cover would encourage the spring growth of the grapes.

But on this chill September day Alberto had done the unthinkable. He had stormed home from the festival, settled himself among the vines with a barrel of wine, and there he remained, drinking and brooding, sunk into misery and despair. No amount of cajoling by Guadalupe and Marie Jose, of yelling and

threatening by Don Pedro, could budge him. He had
abandoned his responsibilities in order to punish
Victoria for her sins, and his family for rallying
behind her. Nothing, not even caring for the grapes
that were his whole life, could pull him out of his
misery and despair.

Though her mother had said she mustn't blame
herself, Victoria knew she was wholly responsible
for Alberto's black mood. Wrapped in a shawl against
the autumn wind that had blown in over the mountains, she watched him from the porch in the deepening dusk. He sat hunched in the vineyard, his back
turned to the family, throwing down glass after glass
of wine. Guadalupe had tried to get him to eat that
morning, but he'd left untouched the meal she'd
brought him. When she came out of the house with
another tray of food for his dinner, Victoria decided
it was up to her to break through his silence and win
his forgiveness.

She took the tray from Guadalupe and walked out
to the vineyard, approaching him as cautiously as
she would a wounded animal. "Papa," she said,
"Grandma made you some food."

He wouldn't look at her. Staring into the gloom
of early evening, he said, "You think the burden of a
family is easy to bear? I didn't ask for this job. But I
accepted it. Everything I did was out of love for
you. Everything."

"You have to eat," she said gently, thinking that
she hadn't asked for the burden of being his child.
She loved him, but she couldn't let him own her, as

if she were a bottle of wine, to be stamped with his label and dispensed with as he chose.

"I give love. And how am I repaid?" he said, his voice rising in anger. "With this . . . this . . ." He turned and pointed contemptuously to her stomach. "This dishonor."

Love wasn't currency that needed paying back, and her baby would not be born into shame. For years she'd held her tongue and lived in fear of his anger. But the cost of obedience was too great, and she'd sacrificed too much to his rage.

She thought of Paul and said, "What you give the vineyard is love. What you give the land is love. What you give us is not love." She remembered the words that had rung through her childhood and raised her voice in imitation of his frequent declarations. "You hate this! You're against that! That's all we ever hear!"

He gulped down another glass of wine in silence.

How to break through his wall of stubbornness, except to tell him the truth? "You're destroying us in the name of love, Papa," she shouted. "Me, Pedro . . . Can't you see you're driving us out? Can't you see that?"

"What happened to respect? That's what I want to know. What about respect?" he demanded. He turned his eyes to the sky, as if he expected the answer to come from the moon and the stars.

She stepped sideways, so he was forced to look at her. "You give respect, you get respect," she said flatly, surprising herself with her boldness.

His response was swift and furious. His hand spun forward and slammed the tray out of her hand. Food, water, utensils flew into the air, spattering all around them. "Get out of here!" he ranted. "Get out! The dishonor you bring to this family . . ."

His frenzied rage was terrifying in its intensity. But she stood her ground. He'd tyrannized her and Pedro for too many years. If she ran from him now, he would spend the rest of his life destroying her.

"Am I the one who uses honor as a weapon to control his family when nothing else works?" she cried. "Am I the one who beat up on the most decent, kind man like some animal? You're the one who brings dishonor to the family, not me! Not anyone else! You!"

She held her breath, waiting for the storm to break.

Too drunk to know she was his daughter and not some apparition he'd conjured up out of the dark recesses of his wine-soaked brain, he screamed, "You have no shame! You whore!"

He was mad, and if she listened to him a minute longer, she'd go mad herself. "I pity you," she said. She left the tray behind for him to pick up the pieces and marched out of the vineyard without another word.

He knew he'd gone too far. He'd wanted to snatch the words back as soon as he'd spat them out at her. But it was too late. He'd seen the anger and hurt in her eyes. And drunk as he was, he knew he'd lost that beautiful little girl who'd adored him more than anyone else in the world. He poured himself more wine, hoping that this would be the glass that would finally eradicate the pain in his heart. Didn't any of them understand what she'd done? A man was nothing without his honor. The Aragons were special, set apart from the rest because they had so much to be proud of. But no more. Victoria had seen to that.

He slumped in his chair. Drought, flooding, phylloxera infestation . . . he'd had his share of overcoming the natural disasters that every vintner faced. But he had no way to deal with—or think about—a daughter who had carelessly, selfishly, destroyed her family's reputation.

Many glasses later, he fell asleep there. On a barrel next to his chair, a kerosene lamp flickered in the darkness, set there by the assistant whom Marie Jose had sent to watch over him. He slept badly and woke up suddenly some time later, parched and sourmouthed from the wine.

"Mr. Aragon?"

Through his stupor he imagined he saw someone standing in front of him.

"I owe you an apology. What I did was wrong."

Alberto roused himself. Who was apologizing to him? The voice was familiar. He peered at the face and saw that it belonged to Paul Sutton, the last man on earth he wanted to see again.

His rage propelled him to his feet. "Get off my land!" he growled.

"My intentions were good," Paul said. "I wanted to protect her."

Alberto stumbled toward him. He could kill this man without a second's thought. "Stay away from her!"

"I can't. She's like air to me. I need her that much. I've come to ask you for her hand in marriage," Paul said.

He would rot in hell before he'd let this bastard come anywhere near Victoria. "You're married already, you son of a bitch!" he snarled. "José!" he shouted to his assistant. "My gun!"

"Don Alberto—"José began.

"Now!" screamed Alberto.

He moved forward on unsteady feet toward Paul, who circled around him, keeping his distance as he pleaded his case. "My marriage was never meant to be. It was the war. It was a mistake. But it's over, annulled. Look!" He thrust some papers at Alberto.

Alberto slapped them away. "You deceived me, in my own house, in my own bed! You made me the fool in front of the world!"

"I'm so sorry. I'm so ashamed of the way I've behaved, and I want to make that up to you, to the family."

Make it up? He'd made Alberto Aragon into the laughingstock of the valley. Nothing could ever make up what he'd done. "To my face! The two of you! Liars!" he shouted, angry enough to tear Paul apart with his bare hands.

"I love her. I want to be with her for the rest of my life. I want to take care of her!"

"José! The gun!" Alberto bellowed.

"Victoria!" Paul yelled into the night.

She woke up to the sound of his voice, calling her name. She thought she was dreaming, until she heard him again. "Victoria!"

Paul was here, at *Las Nubes*. He'd come back for her! She leaped out of bed, rushed downstairs, and hurried out of the house to find him.

"Victoria!" he shouted, moving backward, away from Alberto, who lurched at him with clenched fists.

"Shut up!" Alberto howled. He charged at Paul, punching at the air. "Shut up!"

Paul had the advantage of sobriety. He took one quick step to the left, and Alberto fell forward. He hit the dirt hard, sprawling flat on his face and cursing this outsider who had ruined his life.

"It's not even your child she carries!" he shrieked, scrambling up off the ground.

"It will be if she'll have me!" yelled Paul.

"I'll see you dead first!" Alberto heaved himself up and lunged blindly at Paul. Paul dodged out of his way, and Alberto hit the ground again.

"Victoria!" Paul shouted.

"Paul!" She flung open the door. "Paul!"

He turned toward her voice, leaving himself momentarily unprotected. Alberto grabbed the kerosene lantern from the barrel and swung it hard at Paul's head.

"Paul!" Victoria screamed a warning.

Paul whipped around, saw the lantern coming, and ducked just as it arced overhead. Fiery trails of kerosene streaked across the dry earth.

Alberto couldn't be stopped. He sprang at him, swinging the lantern like a lariat, a madman stalking his prey.

"Papa, stop! Stop!" Victoria cried. She was running, gasping for breath. "I love him! I love him!"

The rest of the family, awakened by the ruckus, came running toward the vineyard.

"You hear her?" Paul shouted, dodging Alberto. "Victoria! I love you!"

"No!" Alberto howled. "No!"

He swung the lantern again as high as he could over Paul's head. This time Paul was ready for him. He grabbed Alberto's arm and spun him around. Alberto stumbled, lost his balance, and fell forward. The lantern flew out of his hand and spiraled across the vineyard. Jets of kerosene sprayed in every direction, sprinkling the vines like drops of rain.

The lantern hit the ground and exploded in a burst of flames. It sent up a shower of sparks that cascaded over the kerosene-soaked vines. There was a sudden flash of bright light, and then a sheet of fire was raging through the vineyard, jumping from vine to vine.

Alberto and the others stood paralysed, stunned by the suddenness of the conflagration. Paul recovered first. He ripped off his shirt, soaked it in the barrel of wine Alberto had been drinking from, and beat it against the flames closest to him. The others immediately followed his example. They stripped off their robes and nightshirts, wet them down with wine, and rushed in to stop the fire from spreading. Heat seared their faces as they slapped at the flames. The fire glowed all around them and under their feet. It had found its perfect medium in the tinder-dry vines. Its flames roared through the vineyard with a heat so intense that finally they were driven back and forced to give up.

Their faces streaked with ash, they retreated to the safety of the road and huddled together, trans-fixed by the sight of the scorching blaze, laying waste to their past, present, and future. It leaped from row to row, fanning out across the acres, sparing nothing. Don Pedro and Guadalupe held hands in stunned silence, while Marie Jose wept quietly on Pedro's shoulder. Victoria buried her head in Paul's chest, and he felt her pain in his heart.

All the way from San Francisco, he'd imagined showing Victoria the annulment papers, then getting down on his hands and knees to propose to her. He'd been so sure the annulment would make it all right with Alberto, and that he'd be welcomed into the family as a son. He stared into the flames. He knew this fire. It had haunted his nightmares. He was that little boy in the too big uniform, destroying everything that mattered.

The fire burned itself out by dawn. All that remained of the vineyard was a smoldering heap of cinders. From the porch where they'd taken refuge, the Aragons mourned the loss of their livelihood, of their hopes and dreams. They couldn't speak. There was nothing anyone could say. They'd lost everything, except one another.

Alberto's grief was thick and black, like the columns of smoke that had risen from the flames. He stood alone, apart from his family. He was too wracked with the guilt of knowing this tragedy was of his making to mourn with them. He couldn't bear to think how much they must hate him—for his stupid pride, his rage, his willfulness. He couldn't forgive himself, so how could they ever forgive him? He'd lost everything that mattered to him. The pain was too much to endure. He wept for the family he'd lost, and for the vines that had sprung from the stock his father had brought with him from Mexico.

"Papa?" Victoria eased herself out of the shelter of Paul's arms. Whatever had passed between them, he was her father, and she still loved him. She walked over and touched him on the shoulder.

"I was afraid of losing you," he said, gazing at the blackened vines. "I am so afraid of losing you, all of you. I didn't know any other way to love."

Tears rolled down his soot-stained face as he turned to her. "Can you teach me?"

Her answer was to put her arms around him in an embrace. She felt his body heave with sobs of grief, and she held more tightly until he was calmer. One by one, the others came to hold him, too. Their arms formed a ring of love around Alberto and

Victoria, as they drew on one another's strength in the face of this catastrophe.

Paul stood back, not wanting to intrude within the intimate circle of the family. The love they shared, and their loyalty, moved him deeply, and made him miss all the more what he'd never had. For a day or two he'd almost felt as if he belonged here with them, in this magical valley that lay hidden now beneath a veil of clouds. The grapes weren't in his blood as they were in theirs, but he felt their loss as keenly as if it were his own.

He remembered the pride and love with which Don Pedro had shown him the shrine where he'd planted the ancient vine from whose roots the other vines had sprung. From the hill where they'd stood, the vineyard had spread out before them in all its glory and splendor.

Nudged by that memory, he stepped off the porch and headed into the mists toward the hill. It was like walking through the landscape of his nightmares. The vineyard, shrouded by the morning mist, looked bleak and devastated. His eyes teared as he squinted into the thick white blanket of smoke that wrapped itself around the seared skeletons of the vines. The smoke seeped into his lungs, and he coughed as he breathed in the tainted air.

He stumbled forward, trying to get his bearings in a land devoid of markers. And then he found what he'd come looking for: the charred remains of the shrine, and below it, the burned vine that had grown up out of Don Pedro's original rootstock. Paul dropped to his knees, sent up a prayer for help, and began digging in the dirt with his hands.

He emerged from the clouds like a wraith, covered in ash and dirt. He was carrying something, cradling it in his arms like a baby. He brought it to Alberto and offered it for inspection.

"Is it alive?" he asked.

It was Don Pedro's rootstock, salvaged from the dirt. Alberto stared at it in amazement, hoping against hope that the miracle he'd prayed for might have been granted him. As the others watched and offered up their own prayers, he gently peeled back the blackened bark. He held it up for them to see. The inner layer of the wood was moist, green, brimming with life.

"It's alive! *Las Nubes* lives!" he said in wonderment.

Don Pedro grabbed Guadalupe and whirled her around in a dance of celebration, while the others shouted in joy and kissed one another.

Alberto took out a knife, sliced off a sliver of the stock, and handed it to Paul. "This is now the root of your life, the root of your family," he said solemnly. "You are bound to this land and to this family by commitment, by honor, by love. Plant it so it will grow."

It was so thin and delicate, almost nothing in his hand. To think that so much could come from so little. . . .

"I don't know how," he said.

He tried to give it back to Alberto, but Alberto shook his head. "Victoria," he said, "help your husband."

She smiled, a joyful, unwavering smile full of love and gratitude, and ran into Paul's arms. It had been a night of so much tragedy, a morning of so many miracles. But out of the tragedy had come the most wonderful and unexpected answer to her prayers . . . she and Paul would be married with her father's blessing. They could build a life together, have children, make their shared dreams come true.

The clouds had lifted. The sun came bursting through the mist. The vineyard would be reborn. The stock would take root, and the vines would sprout again and grow heavy with fruit. The grapes would be harvested, the wine bottled and aged. *Las Nubes* would live on for the next generation, and the one after that.

If ever she'd doubted it, now she knew for certain: She'd found her handsome *caballero*. Just as in her mother's story, he'd remained brave and resolute. He'd never lost hope. And at long last, after many trials and adventures, he'd reached the far shores of the country where his *senorita* awaited him.

The story had a happy ending, as a fairy tale should.